MORE THAN WORDS

HOLIDAY HEARTS

SUSAN SCOTT SHELLEY

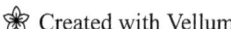 Created with Vellum

CHAPTER ONE

Aidan MacKay prided himself on staying cool under pressure. His army days taught him the importance of an even temper and self-control which served him well in civilian life, too—at work as the head of HR and at play, guarding the net for his hockey team.

But even Zen masters had a limit.

The clock ticking on the wall of his office seemed especially loud, counting down the seconds of an unending day and mocking the plans he'd made to tackle the growing pile on his desk before the workday officially ended. Shaking his head, he pinched the bridge of his nose and then let out a long, slow expulsion of breath.

Waking up to a sick dog, followed by a dead car battery, two employee emergencies, then a showdown with the new payroll company had him clock-watching. As the clock struck three o'clock, he'd barely made a dent in the pile on his desk, wading through seventy-five resumes for only three job openings, two of them temporary. Aidan teetered a breath away from his breaking point.

His head pounded. His mind swam with his never-ending to-do list. And his muscles ached from too many hours hunched over a desk.

Mood darkening fast, he strode into the break room in desperate need of coffee. His friends Hunter and Damon sat at one of the tables, laughing at something on Hunter's phone. Damon glanced up first. "Hey bud. We were wondering where you were."

He grabbed a mug, then reached for the pot of decaf, found it empty, swore, and set it back on the burner. "I've been stuck in resume hell. We received over one hundred responses to the three open Sales positions."

Damon's brows rose. "That many? You remembered to put in the posting that we wanted someone local, that this isn't a work-remotely position?"

He bit his tongue to keep from growling out that he wasn't an idiot. The Kallis Toy Company was known for hiring local and keeping employees long-term. Damon's parents owned the company and went out of their way to make it a family atmosphere. "Everyone who responded claimed to be within a driveable distance to Buffalo. I'm hoping to have the positions filled by the annual general meeting."

That gave him three weeks to find a temporary replacement for an employee out on short-term disability due to a water-skiing accident, a longer term fill-in for an employee on mandatory bed rest due to pregnancy complications, and a permanent replacement for his newest hire who'd quit without offering any notice.

Damon nodded. "I just got out of a meeting with my parents and sister. They want to have everything finished with the company rebranding before the Fourth of July. That gives us six weeks to overhaul the website and all the internal and external audio and videos. Then we can tackle the national campaigns. Kira said she'd set up a meeting with you."

He'd seen Kira's name in the sea of emails flooding his inbox, but it had come in during the hour he'd spent on the phone fighting with the payroll company.

He'd volunteered to step in and help out the short-handed department, but the rebranding had become a thorn in his side. With quick movements, he measured coffee grounds and water into the machine. "Sure. So on top of searching for and then hiring the people we need for that department, I'll see if I can hire a magician to add more hours to my day. It's not happening otherwise. Guess how many of my job duties I accomplished this week. Not a damn thing. Every minute has been eaten up with that project."

Damon's eyes narrowed in the way they did when he was trying to keep a grip on his temper. "You have a problem helping out an understaffed department?"

For the first time in the history of their friendship, Damon appeared irritated that Aidan had sounded off. His best friend never played the VP or I'm-your-boss-card. Open communication all way. Ever since boot camp. He, Damon, and Hunter had served in the same unit. Fought shoulder-to-shoulder in the sweltering heat of Afghanistan. They were closers to him than his brothers. "You know me better than that. It's not the people; it's the situation. I'm not very comfortable acting like a wanna-be advertising genius. If I have to help reword one more commercial, I'm going to put my head through the wall."

"Whoa. Tell us how you really feel." Hunter huffed out a laugh that died on a stony glare from Damon.

Strained silence settled over them, interrupted only by the gurgling of the coffee maker. Aidan walked to the window and leaned against the glass, pinching the bridge of his nose. He had to get himself under control. Of the three of them, he was supposed to be the calm one.

Behind him, a chair scraped against the tile floor. Slow, heavy steps moved further away and then closer until Hunter stood at his elbow, holding out a mug of fresh decaf. "Here."

"Thanks." Aidan gripped the mug and swallowed a mouthful of the fragrant brew. He stared out at the cloudless sky and flowers and greenery that springtime had brought to Western New York, and the Buffalo suburb of Holiday.

He loved his job—usually. And he owed Damon a lot. After their time in the military had ended, Damon had given both Hunter and Aidan jobs at his family's children's toy company—Hunter in IT and him in HR. But more than the job, he'd given him back the family he'd grown to depend on. Regretting the venting, he turned away from the window, ready to meet his best friend's hot-headed temper.

Instead of eyes blazing in anger, Damon regarded him with a weary gaze. Charcoal smudges shadowed below his eyes and a web of premature lines deepened at the corners. He looked exhausted. "I'll take over. Send me the files."

Damn it. That wasn't what he wanted. He should have just kept his mouth shut. "No. Ignore me. I'm sorry for complaining. I can get Angie to help."

His assistant would be returning from her vacation in a few days. Things wouldn't be so bad by then, right?

He crossed to the table and sat, trying and failing to ignore the uncharacteristic awkwardness circulating between them. After a moment, Hunter launched into a story about something that had happened in the IT department. Aidan laughed at the appropriate times, but his focus remained on Damon and his wooden laugh and subdued expression.

Finally, he couldn't take it anymore. Feeling like a jerk, he refilled his mug and returned to his office. Why had he vented? He didn't feel any better and only gave Damon one more headache.

He hunkered down and pushed through the remaining resumes, jotting notes on a few that could work out. Email after email appeared in his inbox and frustration mounted again. Blood pounded in his temples. He forwarded what could wait into Angie's inbox, and then glared at the rest.

"Might as well get started," he mumbled, scrolling down the list of unread messages.

A name popped out at him from the mass. A pleasant surprise. He lifted his fingers away from the keyboard and sat back, staring at the screen.

Skye Galen.

The voiceover artist had been working with the company for the past six months, voicing sales training tutorials and workplace safety videos. Her friendly emails always made him smile. He closed his eyes and leaned back in his chair and hit *play* on the sound file.

Her voice glided out of the speakers, enticing him to open his eyes as if he expected her to be standing in front of his desk. Calming. Soothing. Like a spring rainfall cooling his hot skin. His heartbeat slowed. Breathing eased and his taut muscles loosened.

The recording ended all too quickly.

Surprise and wonder stole through him. He sat up straight, staring at the sound file on the screen, and hit repeat. Her voice flowed once again.

Wonderfully modulated.

Slightly husky.

Completely sexy.

Her voice contained magic. Real magic. No recording had ever affected him like that before.

He hit repeat again. And again. Repeat. Repeat. Repeat.

Perfection.

Her voice possessed the same relaxing effect as an hour's worth of yoga, or several minutes of deep breathing, or time spent playing with his dog. Instant, utter peace. He'd listened to her recordings before, as they'd come in during the last few months, but none had ever affected him so deeply. Then again, he hadn't been in a massive mess of stress and frustration before, either.

Heartbeat quickening, he clicked on the link for her website below her email signature. A background in shades of blue as peaceful as her voice, countless testimonials, and demos showcasing a broad range of projects, including a few for Kallis, filled his screen. Her *About* page spoke of a previous career in radio before pursuing voiceovers full-time. He'd known she liked music; they'd had an interesting email exchange on rock bands when he'd mentioned his hockey team listened to eighties hair metal bands in the locker room before games.

He clicked through each page. Unfortunately, none had a photo of Skye. He would have loved a face to place with the name and voice. They'd emailed back and forth quite a bit during her last few projects. He'd learned that she loved scary movies, Italian food, and lucky for him, hockey—even though they rooted for two rival professional teams. Hell, he knew more about her than the last three women he'd dated—combined. And that last date had been long enough ago to give him pause.

She was funny, sweet, and now, he was eager, more than eager, to get to know her even better.

Screw it—why wait?

He jabbed his fingers at his phone's keypad and dialed the number listed in her email.

Two rings later, she answered, "Hello?"

"Skye?"

"Yes?"

"It's Aidan. Aidan MacKay. With Kallis Toys."

"Aidan, hello. It's nice to hear from you." Her voice flowed around him like a gentle breeze. The way she said his name... He wanted her to say it again.

He shifted the phone to his other hand and relaxed against the back of his chair. "I wanted to let you know how happy we've been with you."

"Thank you. I'm so glad. I love working with you. Kallis is one of my favorite clients."

An urge need to see her consumed him. Hearing her voice live only heightened his craving for more. Nothing short of a face to face interaction would do. "I'd love to meet you sometime."

"Yes, well—" A blast of hard rock music echoed through the speaker, drowning out her voice. Two feminine voices mixed in with the rioting notes before he heard a door close. Quiet returned.

He glanced at the phone, wishing he could see her through it. "Uh... Are you okay?"

"I'm sorry. My sister is here visiting, and she accidentally turned on my sound system. In hindsight, having a universal remote wasn't a smart decision."

"Good taste in music. Can't go wrong with The Fury. Great band."

"I'm so embarrassed—not about the band—I saw them in concert twice, and they were amazing. I'll be hiding the remote from Terri for the rest of her stay." Skye spoke louder, over the other voice profusely apologizing in the background, strong enough to penetrate the closed door.

He chuckled, more relaxed that he'd felt in ages. "Don't worry about it. I'll let you get back to your sister."

"Wait. Did you need something specific?"

She seemed flustered. And he didn't want to continue the conversation when she had a captive audience. "It can wait. I'll be in touch with more projects soon."

"I look forward to them." Her voice softened, and he smiled.

He was still grinning like a fool a full minute later.

A single knock sounded on his door, and then Damon entered his office. "Got a minute?"

"I—" He straightened in his chair and pointed to the screen. "Skye Galen is the voiceover artist we've been using for the sales training and the workplace safety videos. I know we had that guy from Buffalo voice a few of the health benefits presentations when Skye wasn't available, but she's the one I want as the voice for the rebranding."

"Sure you aren't jumping the gun just to get this over with?"

"No, man. I'm serious."

"Yeah? Let *me* hear." Damon sat on the edge of the desk, head cocked to the side, as Skye's voice filled the room. He nodded but stayed silent when the recording ended.

Aidan had to restrain himself from replaying it yet again. "She's reliable, fast, and perfect for what we need."

"Sounds good to me. I think she'd be great to voice our television commercials, too. We'll have to see how she works out on the other projects first." He folded his arms across his chest and leaned closer. "I know helping out Sales with this project has dumped a lot of work on you. I appreciate you stepping in and taking this on. Since you're swamped, I'm sure Kira can take over and—"

"No, no, no. I'm a team player. Your sister has enough on her plate right now with all the changes in her department. I'm happy to help out. I'll be the liaison between Skye and Kira." Aidan closed the sound file and stood, ready to fight for the right to keep the contact with Skye. "I'll need to work with Skye when we do the rest of the workplace safety videos, the new employee orientation, and the phone system re-recordings anyway. So it makes sense to give her just one contact here for everything. Less confusing that way."

Brow raised, Damon stood and mirrored his stance. "You seem pretty eager considering the bitching you were doing earlier. What changed?"

He shrugged, not wanting to admit he was too

intrigued to pass her along to someone else to handle. Plus, he did feel sorry about what happened in the break room. "After all you've done for me, this is the least I can do."

His best friend slowly shook his head. "Normally, I'd believe the *I'm doing this for my old Army buddy* reason, but not this time. You're acting weird."

A soft ping alerted him to a new message in his inbox. From Skye. He wanted to be alone when he read it. "It's getting near quitting time, and we have a hockey game in an hour so you should probably go clear up your desk. It wouldn't look good if our team captain is late."

"Okay. Have it your way. But I will find out." With a confident smirk, Damon exited the room.

At least things between them seemed fine again. Aidan sank onto his chair. Heartbeat ticking faster, he opened the email.

Hi Aidan,

I'm so sorry about what happened when you called. My sister apologizes too. I've confiscated the remote and the only device she is allowed to touch for the remainder of her visit is the coffee maker. As always, I look forward to working with you on future projects.

I'll be here whenever you need me,

Skye

A grin spread across his face. He returned to her website and played the various demos. Her voice changed from friendly to informative to concerned, but each one had the same effect on his system—utter peace.

He'd give anything to bottle that up. And maybe, with Skye, he'd find something more than the words filling the air.

CHAPTER TWO

Skye slipped out of her recording booth and carried the script and water bottle to her computer. She stopped the recording software, performed a quick check on the sound quality then saved the file. Editing the audio was the longest part of the process. Thankfully, she hadn't made too many flubs while recording. Not every company had scripts that were as well-written as those from The Kallis Toy Factory, with sentences that flowed easily when spoken out loud.

She'd told Aidan as much in her last email.

Shrieks of laughter bubbled through the window, and she leaned back in her chair to look out. The kids in the yard next door were jumping into their pool, care-free and happy. She hadn't been to a pool or beach in years. Summer used to be her favorite season, but now she dreaded it. Hot weather made wearing extra layers difficult.

She'd chosen Holiday, New York because she

wanted a place that had long winters and lots of snow. The total opposite of Miami. The perfect place to stay bundled up and hidden beneath chunky sweaters and scarves for several months out of the year. But spring and summer came to Western New York, too. Maybe she should have chosen Alaska. Or Antarctica.

She tugged her sweater tighter around her torso and returned her attention to her desk.

A new email from Aidan popped up. She looked forward to his emails more than any other client's correspondence. Over the past six months, she'd learned he had a sense of humor, played hockey, ran in the mornings, and had a Golden Retriever named Chance.

It was the closest thing to a relationship that she'd had in two years.

Hi Skye,

I hope you're having a good day and that your sister hasn't ruined the coffee maker too. Mine started out with Chance's leash breaking during my morning run. He took off after a squirrel and wouldn't come back. Picture five guys from my running group trying to chase him down. He thought it was the best game ever. I'm happy to report both dog and squirrel were eventually recovered unharmed.

Laughing, she continued to read.

Anyway, attached is another script for the sales training. Just do what you always do—the tone and pacing are perfect.

She nodded, pleased, and glanced at his last line.

Are you available to video chat tomorrow? There's

*something I need to ask you, and I'd like to talk about it
more in-person than just an email or phone call.*

Her breath caught in her chest, and a chill crept over
her skin.

He wanted to talk to her.

Not another phone call.

Face to face.

Tremors rocked her stomach. Needing to steady her
breathing, she pushed away from her desk. Why
couldn't he just ask the question in an email?

Reminding herself that the face-to-face aspect
shouldn't be an issue didn't work. Some of her clients
wanted to talk, either by phone or video chat when
discussing a project, and she always accommodated
them, even though doing so caused trepidation. But
Aidan's request caused extra waves of stress.

She liked him, and she wasn't ready to have that
illusion shattered.

Maybe he'd believe her computer's camera was
broken… Or maybe she could just upload her site's
logo, and he could see that image instead of seeing her
live. But he'd said he'd wanted a more in-person meeting, so using the logo seemed to be the coward's
way out.

Loud footsteps preceded her sister's entrance into
the room. Terri swept in, holding her phone and wearing
an exasperated expression. "I just got off the phone with
Mom."

A sinking feeling filled Skye's stomach. Phone calls

with her mom always caused the same reaction. "Let me guess, I was the topic of conversation?"

Terri nodded and rolled her eyes. "The whole time, she kept harping on how it's eighty degrees and sunny in Holiday today, how she hoped you stayed covered up if you went outside or if not, and remembered to slather sunscreen all over. I think she mentioned the words burns, scars, and donor sites about twenty times. Some things never change. She also didn't ask much about me. I'm beginning to get a complex that I'm not the favorite child."

"Fabulous." Skye bit out the word, then grabbed her water bottle and downed half the contents. She barely resisted giving into the urge to throw it across the room. As much as she loved her parents, they were always reminding her of the scars, talking about the burns, and treating her like she'd just been released from the hospital. Another reason why she'd chosen to move a plane ride away.

Terri pocketed her phone. "I reminded her that you're thirty-two, not twelve and that you know the drill when it comes to that stuff. She was also making noises about coming up here and spending the summer taking care of you."

"No. *No way.* We'd drive each other crazy." She loved her mom, but not the smothering. "I don't need anyone taking care of me. It's been two years. I'm fine."

"If you were fine, then you wouldn't be hiding out at home all the time." Her sister's voice took on the *I'm older and therefore wiser* tone. For the first time, Skye resented Terri's know-it-all attitude, made worse since the fire.

She tugged the sleeve of her sweater over her hand and wandered back to the window. "I don't sit home all the time."

Going out for groceries once a week, counted, right? Even if it was at midnight when the store was mostly empty. Working from home meant she could run other errands during off-peak hours, too—always carefully made up and covered up.

"Fine, then tell me about some friends you have here or guys you're dating, Ms. Social Butterfly."

"Well…" She couldn't lie. She talked to her sister on the phone at least twice a week. Terri knew there weren't any friends or guys in the picture.

"Please. In the three days I've been here, we haven't gone out once." Terri folded her arms across her chest and raised one sculpted brow. "I'm leaving tomorrow and my experience of this area was contained to the cab ride from the airport."

"I thought we were having fun just hanging out here. Plus, I've had some work to do, projects to record." She glanced around her office.

"Speaking of projects to record, have you heard anything back from the guy I accidentally blasted with the music yesterday? You told him I apologized, right?"

"Yes, and yes. He just sent me another script. And he wants to video chat with me… probably about a project."

"From what I could hear, his voice sounded sexy. Have you ever looked him up?"

Of course, she'd looked him up. Curiosity had gotten the better of her one day early into their initial recording contract. She'd reasoned that knowing more about the companies she worked with was a smart business decision. "Want to see him?"

She clicked on his company website, and then Aidan's profile in the directory. His photo filled the upper left corner of the page. Stylishly short brown hair so dark it was nearly black. Straight nose. Good bone structure. But his eyes drew her in. Chocolate brown, they smiled back from his image, as if only for her. There was a steadiness about him that called to her.

Up until yesterday, she'd spent six months wondering what type of voice he had.

Now she knew.

Deep, quiet, and calming.

With a sigh, she minimized the screen.

Speculating on Aidan was a waste of time.

She would always be alone.

"Whoa. He's mega-hot. Bordering on melting." Terri fanned herself.

"Settle down there, married lady." Skye smiled in spite of her mini pity-party. She missed having her sister around all the time. Not enough to move back to Miami, just enough for it to hurt when she left.

Terri rested a hip on her desk. "You like this guy. I can tell. Ask him out."

She snorted. "Right. Because the world is made of hearts and rainbows and happy endings."

"You need to get out more. You're becoming a recluse. You can't hide away forever."

"Easy for you to say." Her sister was beautiful. Terri didn't have people staring at her and whispering, or little kids pointing and asking what was wrong with her chest, arm, and cheek. Terri didn't have to deal with men turning away, interest cooling, once they glimpsed the left side of her body.

"Look, I know the last thing you need is Mom coming up here and fussing over you, but if you don't start living, then I might move in myself."

"Your kids and husband would miss you."

"You're my sister and my best friend. I'm worried about you. Before the fire, you were always the most vibrant person in any room. I know the aftermath was a nightmare, but now, you're like a ghost of your former self. You fought for so long… What's the point in living if you're going to be hidden away?"

"It's hard." Skye forced the whisper through her dry throat. She crossed to the window on the opposite side of the room and peered into the sun-drenched front yard. Plenty of people were strolling by enjoying the afternoon. If she stepped outside, all of her focus would be, as always, on making sure her scars stayed concealed. "I'm so lonely. But I hate the stares and the pity."

"You need to get past that."

"I know." She was sick of her self-imposed isolation, but breaking through it seemed impossible. "I want to, but the thought of going out there, putting myself out there, is terrifying. Paralyzing." Especially when she thought of the encounters she'd had so far.

"I'm so sorry." Terri's arms surrounded her in a hug.

Skye sniffled and swallowed hard against the tears threatening to form. "Don't tell Mom and Dad about anything I said, okay? They worry enough."

"I promise on one condition. Do something that scares you. Please. For me. I know it's hard, but you deserve so much more than to be confined to a house for the rest of your life."

Terri had been there for her every step of the way. From hours in the hospital, both in the burn unit and then for every surgery, through her recovery, to helping her move to Holiday, and for running interference with their parents. She would do anything for her sister.

Skye nodded and pulled back. The email from Aidan and his request called to her like a beacon. She could do it. For Terri. For herself. She had to try. "I promise."

CHAPTER THREE

Sunlight streamed in through the windows of his home office, bright and clean. Aidan paced the length, counting down the minutes. After six months of emails, of listening to every recording that came in, the mystery of what Skye looked like was about to be revealed. Tall, short, blonde, brunette, the specifics didn't matter—as long as he knew what to picture when he thought about her. Because he thought about her a lot.

Anticipation had fueled him all morning, more potent than the caffeine he'd given up. He sat behind his desk and smoothed his hand down the front of his shirt. It may have been a Saturday, and he may have been at home, but he'd dressed like he was going to the office in a light blue button-down shirt and dark pants. No matter what, he represented Kallis and wanted to make a good impression. He looked at Chance. "How do I look?"

The Golden Retriever trotted over, licked his hand and then settled on the floor next to his chair.

"I'll take that as approval." He laughed and logged onto the video chat site.

Chance rubbed his head against Aidan's calf. He reached down and patted the soft fur. The dog had been with him for the past few years. At the suggestion of his therapist, he'd adopted the docile pet. Not officially a therapy dog, Chance still sensed his PTSD episodes and would rouse him from horrific nightmares. Man's best friend indeed.

An alert sounded when Skye logged in. He clicked to initiate a chat, and suddenly the screen came alive with her image. Long, honey blonde hair cascaded over part of her face and flowed in front of her shoulder. Large brown eyes sparkled and soft pink lips curved in a smile. She was beautiful. She wore a gauzy gray scarf and a white long-sleeved sweater that teased at her curves. Her desk hid the rest of her. His fingers itched to reach through the screen and take her hand. "Hi."

"It's nice to meet you." One hand lifted to her scarf. No rings adorned her fingers. But it was her right hand, not left. The idea that she might belong to someone else sent a streak of jealousy through him.

He forced that thought aside. "I know you said in your original email that you're within driving distance of Holiday. How drivable?"

"Actually, I live here."

"No way." He grinned and leaned closer to the screen. "That's even better."

Chance jumped up, paws on Aidan's lap and head

on Aidan's desk. He ruffled the dog's fur. "Apparently, someone wants to be introduced. This is Chance."

Her eyes softened. "He's beautiful. I guess he's recovered from his squirrel chase?"

"Shh." He laid his hands over Chance's ears and lowered his voice. "We never say the "s" word in front of him. He goes nuts."

They shared a grin, and he kicked himself for not making the video chat suggestion earlier.

"So, what did you want to talk to me about?" She straightened her shoulders, and her lips pressed together. He could understand her subtle wariness, but he didn't like that he'd inadvertently put her on the defensive.

"Nothing bad. I hope it's good news to you. It is to us. We're rebranding and would love for you to be the voice of the company. Kallis, I mean."

"The voice of the company? Really?" That bright smile was back, happiness beaming out of her.

"Everyone is impressed by your work. Your voice rocks. There's plenty of projects to come, like work-place safety announcements, audio for the welcome video on the company website, the phone system. The big thing is the voiceovers for our nationwide television commercials and campaigns, the web and radio ads, too. We'll be working together for a long time."

"That's amazing. I'd love that. Thank you so much for thinking I'd be a good fit."

"You're perfect." He smiled while hers widened even more. She'd agreed, and that meant a long-term relationship. Good for Kallis Toys and good for him.

"There's one other thing—well, two actually. Our annual general meeting is next Friday, the tenth, at two o'clock. We'd like you to voice one of the presentations."

"Of course. No problem."

"And, we want you to voice it here. Live."

The smile fell from her face, and her eyes rounded. "Live… at the meeting?"

"We'd like to introduce you when we discuss rebranding and thought this would be a great way. Instead of being in a booth, you'll be reading it at the front of the room. You'll get to meet everyone that way. Our creative team will be able to speak with you then, too."

She pressed her lips together and then nodded, but she looked nervous as hell. "I can do that."

"Great. It's important to my—"

The loud vroom of a sports car drowned out his words. His head snapped toward the window and, though he saw the silver racer streak by. The car backfired gunshot loud and emitted smoke. Immediately, old memories consumed him.

No longer seeing his computer or desk, he hunched low in his seat, squeezing his head between his hands. His lungs seized. His stomach lurched.

Dizziness sped through him like a tornado. The room spun wildly, a blur of memory and reality. His head filled with the explosions of hot artillery and images of wounded soldiers littering an arid landscape flashed fast before his eyes. In the distance, he heard the piercing bark of a dog. His dog. Chance. He grasped the edges of the desk and wheezed in a long breath.

"Aidan?" Skye's concerned face sharpened into view. She leaned closer to the screen. "Aidan?"

"Sorry… Some noises… trigger… my…" *Breathe.* He couldn't breathe. Cold sweat covered his skin. He gripped the arms of the chair with his clammy hands, his heartbeat thundered louder than the engine. "Just keep talking to me. Please."

Without question or the slightest hint of judgment, she did. "I'm here with you, Aidan. Don't be afraid. Concentrate on the sound of my voice. Close your eyes. Look to your center. And breathe."

He closed his eyes, letting her encouraging words flow around him and concentrated on moving the air in and out of his lungs.

Soft fur brushed across his limp hands as Chance jumped into his lap. Aidan groaned under the weight while the dog adjusted himself, paws hanging off both ends of his lap as if not wanting to block Aidan's view of the screen. Hands shaking, he cradled the dog, grateful for the canine comfort. Skye's voice continued to stream through the speakers, wrapping around him. Her tone and cadence eased the stranglehold of his panic.

Finally, his breathing flowed, regular and even. His heart resumed its normal beating. Hands steady, he opened his eyes.

Skye stopped mid-sentence and reached her hand toward the screen. "Are you okay?"

His face grew impossibly hot. Chance pressed closer again, licking his chin. Concentrating on the dog gave him a moment to compose himself. He settled Chance on his lap and then met her gaze. "Thanks. Sorry. I, ah, some loud noises are a trigger for me. They pull me back into some memories and…."

"It's all right." Her tone gentle, she played with one of the ends of her scarf. Her right hand twisted the material. "I understand. Completely. But do you have a way of handling it? You know—when someone's not around?"

Something about the way she spoke and her expression made him want to ask how she understood, to see if maybe she suffered the same or knew someone who did. He wanted to ask, but he'd never press. People needed to open up in their own time. "I do yoga every day and deep breathing exercises when something sets me off, plus I have Chance. All that helps a lot. But not as much as your voice. I have a confession to make. This will probably sound strange, but I've been using your sound files to help me calm down."

Her brows rose. For a moment she didn't say anything. He felt like an idiot. He shouldn't have told her. But then she treated him to another of those brilliant smiles. "I'm glad I'm able to help you."

Maybe she didn't think he was odd for doing it. Maybe she'd give him—the real him—a chance. "So, can I take you to dinner as a thank you, after the meeting next week? There's a great Italian place not too far from Kallis. We could get to know each other better."

Her lips opened and then closed. Creases formed in her forehead as she pulled back from the screen. Her right hand tugged on the end of her hair. He recognized panic easily enough. "I... I... I'm sorry, I have to go."

That fast, her image disappeared. Their chat ended.

An emptiness welling in his gut, he stared at the black screen. What the hell just happened?

Three hours later, as Aidan stood minding the net for the Blades, he couldn't stop thinking about Skye. The possible reasons for her abrupt end to their conversation flew by him as fast as the pucks he should have been stopping.

He'd come on too strong. She wasn't interested. She didn't want the emotional drama of dealing with him. She didn't want to get involved with a client. She wasn't single. Thought after thought after thought...

At the start of the third period, Hunter, on defense, circled toward him. "You sure you're all right?"

Behind the safety of his mask, he nodded and waved his stick. All of his teammates were giving him questioning glances—had been since goal number three in the first period. Unlike professional leagues, the teams in his rec league didn't have a back-up goalie whose only job was being back-up goalie. If something happened to Aidan, one of the other guys would have to strap on the pads and take his place, but that would leave one of the skating positions without a necessary replacement. And if he took himself out or got pulled, the rules dictated that he couldn't play fill-in for another position. He'd never handicap his teammates that way. He'd stay in as long as he could.

But when goal number six flew by him, he was ready to pull himself. He couldn't deny he was a detriment to his team.

Damon signaled for a time-out and headed his way. He expected the captain to tell him to hang up his skates. Instead, his friend stopped and took a shot of water from the bottle on the top of the net while the rest of his teammates gathered around him. "We have five minutes left, and we're down by three. We can mount a comeback if everyone does their job."

Aidan winced as most of the team glanced at him. "Sorry, guys. Timing's off."

Hunter shook his head. "Some of those goals were my fault. I should be playing better defense."

"Nope." Aidan waved his glove to stop the rest of the guys from taking the blame for him. "They're all on me."

"We win and lose together, boys." Damon tapped his stick against Aidan's pads. "Now let's take back the game."

The whistle sounded. Play resumed.

And three more goals found their way by Aidan before the final buzzer sounded.

The Blades lost nine to three.

Nine goals. He'd never let in nine goals before.

He was the last player off the ice. When he entered the locker room, the chatter fell silent. He set his stick and helmet on the bench. "Sorry guys. My fault. Drinks are on me tonight."

Most of the team had been together for the last few years, playing in winter, spring, fall, and summer hockey leagues. They were like an extended family. He hated letting them down.

He showered and dressed and gathered his equipment. Everyone gave him a wide berth and the locker room quickly emptied. When he stepped outside into the warm early evening air, he found his core support, his friends he loved like family, waiting for him on the front steps of the building.

Damon's sister Kira sat next to Hunter. Her hand rubbed her fiance's thigh, helping him massage where bullet holes had torn into him all those years ago. Aidan wanted what Kira and Hunter had. He was thirty-five years old and tired of being alone. But damn it, he'd blown his chance with Skye.

Damon handed him a bottle of water. "Don't let it get to you, man. We all have off games."

"Yeah." After hugging Kira hello, he set his equipment bag down and sat between Hunter and Damon, not ready to head to the pub and deal with happy, smiling people.

Hunter nudged his arm. "The last time you let in more than four goals was when you had walking pneumonia and shouldn't have even been playing. What's up?"

"Skye and I had that video call today to talk about the rebranding, and while we were talking a damn car backfired outside my house."

"Oh, shit." Damon's hand came to rest on his shoulder. "I'm sorry."

"Aidan." Kira reached over and squeezed his hand.

"I asked Skye to keep talking to me. Told her that her voice soothes me. That I'd been using her sound files to calm down."

"Wow." Hunter raised his brows and turned to face him. "I didn't know that."

"Me neither." Damon squeezed his shoulder again. Then, his expression lightened and he slapped Aidan's chest and grinned. "That's why you were so eager to keep her to yourself for the project. Mystery solved."

He rubbed the spot over his heart. "Yeah, well. That doesn't matter much anymore."

Kira gently squeezed his hand again before letting go. "This sounds like more than you being uncomfortable because it happened in front of a client. You like her."

"I think I blew my chance with her. After I'd told her… you know… I asked her to dinner. As a thank you. And so we could get to know each other. Fuck. She looked panicked. And then she ended the call faster than those slap shots firing by me today."

"You didn't blow your chance." Damon, their resident fixer, slowly stood and stretched. "She's coming to the meeting. We'll make sure to put in a good word for you."

"Yeah. Of course." Hunter clapped him on the back. "You haven't shown real interest like this in a long time."

Not since he'd returned home, actually. He shrugged, tried to pretend it wasn't important, that he wasn't lonely, that he didn't care if things worked out or not.

If he'd blown it with Skye, at least he still had his friends.

That might have to be enough.

CHAPTER FOUR

Two days after the video call, Skye braved the mall, late enough to avoid the early mall walkers and early enough to avoid the lunch crowd. Her favorite sweaters were a little too casual to wear to a business meeting, as were the jeans, yoga pants, and T-shirts that made up her work-from-home attire. She needed a new suit.

She bypassed the fun watermelon pinks, aqua blues, and siren reds for the blend into the background pale gray option, and picked up a handful of blouses on her way to the dressing room.

Her heart started pounding the moment the door closed at her back. Full-length mirrors were too honest. She ignored looking until she'd fully pulled on the first outfit.

Changing clothes had mussed her hair, revealing the uneven skin on her cheek. The first blouse hit too low on her chest, showcasing bumpy, craggy skin. Options two and three weren't much better. She'd definitely need a scarf. The arms of the suit jacket lay perfectly at her wrist, but that couldn't hide the scar covering the back of her left hand.

No matter what she did, she couldn't entirely mask what had happened.

Tears burned into her vision, melting her image in the mirror into a blur. Shoulders shaking, she pressed her lips together to hold in her sobs as hot tears tracked down her cheeks.

Memories of countless rejections, of averted eyes and long-winded excuses, of gasps and insensitive comments, mocked her reflection.

Why would Aidan be any different?

Breath heaving, she sank onto the cushioned seat and searched her purse for a tissue.

No way could she sit through a dinner with Aidan. Not with the way he'd looked at her without knowing the extent of the scars hiding beneath her clothes.

He apparently suffered from PTSD, but he also apparently lived a regular life. A good life, with friends and family and a sweet dog. He had coping mechanisms. She did not.

And as handsome as he was, she couldn't imagine him not having a long line of people interested in him.

The best thing to do was to cancel, to beg off the meeting. The company didn't need her to be physically present. If they still wanted her to voice the presentation, she could do that from the comfort of her recording booth and send Aidan the file—the way she had for every other project.

With wooden movements, she changed back into her sweater, scarf, and jeans and smoothed her hair until it draped into place. Then she set the clothes on the rack outside the dressing room and walked, head down, to her car. The heat hit her, tempting her to remove the sweater. Glaring at the A/C, she turned it up all the way, took a deep breath, and dialed his number.

He answered on the third ring. "Aidan MacKay."

She closed her eyes at the deep, smooth voice. "Hi, it's Skye."

"Hey," his voice warmed until she was sure a smile had spread across his face. "How are you?"

"Uh… Listen, about the meeting, I don't think I'll be able to come—"

"Can you hold on a minute please?" Aidan's voice cut in. Behind his voice, another man's rumbled, accompanied by something rustling. He hadn't put her on hold but likely had cupped his hand over the mouthpiece. After a few moments of muddled conversation, he came back on the line. "My boss, Damon Kallis, the VP of our company, is here. He'd like to say hello, so I'm going to put the call on speaker."

The VP? Yikes. She nodded before remembering that he couldn't see her. "Okay, sure."

"Skye?" A voice three shades rougher than Aidan's came through the line. "Damon Kallis here. We've been very happy with your work."

"It's nice to meet you. I've really enjoyed voicing the projects for your company."

"We're looking forward to seeing you on Friday. My

parents, who own the company, are very excited to meet you. This company is known for having a family atmosphere, and we always hire locally. They like having personal relationships with each person who has any hand in any part of our business."

"I see." But she didn't, really.

"I know Aidan has spoken to you about becoming the voice of our company. We want that person to be able to come in and work with us here on a semi-regular basis."

Work there? Aidan hadn't mentioned that. But then again, he'd experienced the trigger episode right as he was telling her about being the voice. "But I have a studio—"

"Don't worry, we have one here, too, and we're pretty proud of it. We'll be doing the audio recording and filming for the commercials here. Our creative team has a lot of ideas and having you in-house for the recording would make things easier."

She finally understood what he wasn't saying. If she didn't show up to the meeting, she'd still have to show up at the factory if she wanted to keep the job. And if she didn't want to show up at the factory, then she could kiss the job goodbye.

Freelance work wasn't a steady constant. Her work-load and income fluctuated monthly. She couldn't guar-antee when she'd land a big contract again, and she couldn't afford to lose out on this one. Aidan's company paid well. Extremely well. And promptly—which was more than she could say about some of her other clients.

All of those projects from Kallis would go a long way toward making up for the lean months.

"So, you were saying something about the meeting?" he prompted.

"Uh, yes." Heart pounding, she pressed a hand to her chest. "I'm looking forward to it."

"Perfect. We are too." He had to be smiling; his voice sounded too confident and satisfied. "I'll have Aidan forward you the presentation so you can familiarize yourself with it beforehand. And, Ms. Galen, I'm really looking forward to meeting you, too."

"I am, too, Skye." Aidan's voice warmed her to her core.

She stammered her goodbye, then ended the call. What the hell was she going to do now?

Leaning back in her seat, she rested her head and looked out the window for an answer.

———

One week after her phone call with Aidan and Damon, Skye sat in her car in the parking lot of Kallis Toy Factory. Nerves jangled her system, and her hands shook. It was almost time to meet Aidan. She'd barely eaten breakfast and hadn't been able to stomach lunch.

She gave her reflection another critical scan. Hair in a deep side part draped across her forehead, angled across her face, and lay in front of her left shoulder, concealing her cheek. Makeup carefully layered and applied, she'd added extra highlights to draw attention to her eyes and away from her lips and cheek. The pale pink scarf wound just-so, covered any skin her shirt and suit jacket might reveal. She'd dabbed makeup on her left hand and planned to hide it behind her purse as much as possible.

Her phone chimed with a *good luck* text from her sister. She'd called Terri after her conversation with Damon, and her amazing big sister had talked her into going back to the store, and had stayed on the call and helped her select a white cap-sleeved top that had a boat-neck collar, the scarf, and the pale gray suit.

She grabbed her papers with the presentation script and her purse and walked across the parking lot. Thankfully, zero breezes stirred the air. All she had to do was get through the presentation. Aidan had sent her three scripts that week, but hadn't again mentioned going to dinner. Maybe he wanted to forget the whole thing.

Maybe he'd found someone else.

A shard of disappointment cracked the shield she'd been determined to hold.

She rolled her shoulders and stepped into the cool lobby. Aidan had mentioned he'd meet her there, but she hadn't expected him to be waiting for her.

He stood by the reception desk and a friendly smile broke across his face. She smiled back despite her nerves. He strode to her, confident in a charcoal gray suit, and extended his hand. "Skye. We meet at last."

"Aidan." She placed her palm against his and curled her fingers around his big hand. He was tall, easily six foot three. At five-foot-nine, she appreciated height. Heels brought her eye-level with his mouth. She tilted her head back just enough to meet his gaze and still keep her cheek concealed. She'd been right about those cocoa brown eyes, they drew her right in.

"I'm glad you could make it." His voice, that deep, smooth, wonderful tone, called to her, and something in her soul echoed back.

She stepped closer. "I appreciate the opportunity."

He still held her hand, standing a hair closer than business-appropriate, with that sexy smile fixed on his face. "We'll be getting started in a few minutes. Can I get you anything—coffee, water?"

"I'm good." She had enough caffeine in her to last for days. "Maybe a bottle of water for when I'm giving the presentation."

Someone called his name and then two men approached, one with dark hair, the other a sandy blond. Aidan released his grip and gestured first to the dark-haired man. "This is Damon Kallis, VP of Kallis Toys. You spoke on the phone last week."

"It's a pleasure." Damon shook her hand. "As I said on the phone, we're very happy with your work. I'm glad Aidan found you."

"Thank you." She glanced between the three men, all as tall as trees.

Aidan then pointed to the blond. "And this is Hunter York. He works in IT and will be the first name called out if something goes wrong with the presentations today."

"Yep." Blue eyes twinkling, Hunter shook her hand. "Without me, this whole thing would fall apart."

"The scary part is, he's right." Damon glanced at his watch. "Time to head up. Meeting's going to start soon."

They stepped onto a crowded elevator. Squeezed between Aidan and the wall, she could only breathe in his fresh, clean linen scent and feel his heat. A gust of air blew as the doors opened, tossing her hair away from her face and ruffling her scarf.

No. Her hand flew to her hair as they exited the car. Heartbeat ticking faster, she rushed to smooth everything back into place. Her elbow hit his arm, and he twisted toward her. Wishing for a mirror, she shifted away from him and dropped her left hand to her side before he could see it.

He stopped walking and leaned down, forehead creasing in concern. "Hey, are you okay? You look so nervous. Don't worry, it's a friendly group. You'll do great."

She latched onto his assumption. "It's been a while since I spoke in front of a large crowd. This will be pretty different from reading in the comfort of my solitary recording booth. Plus, I can edit out the mistakes there. No way to erase any flubs here."

"Once you start talking, no one will care if you make a few mistakes. I love listening to your voice, but then I've told you that before."

Nerves shifted into awareness. All at once, his expression reminded her of when he'd confessed to using her sound files to calm down. "Aidan."

Applause rang out from the room down the hall. He glanced over his shoulder. "We better go. They've already started."

The meeting room was huge, sun-drenched with two walls of windows, and filled to capacity. Over two hundred people crowded into seats.

Damon stood at the podium in front of the room, speaking as different pie charts and colorful graphs filled the screen behind him.

Aidan handed Skye a bottle of water from the two he'd palmed on the way in and led her along the perimeter to seats in the third row. Skye settled next to him, making sure to keep him on her right side. He leaned close throughout Damon's speech to give her little bits of information, helping her feel included. His voice, rumbling in her ear, sent delicious zings down her spine.

Finally, Damon announced her name. Aidan's hand rested on her arm for an instant and he whispered, "Good luck," in her ear.

Clutching her water bottle and papers, she made her way across the room and then faced the sea of people staring back at her. Damon finished his speech about rebranding, then read the brief bio that Skye had on her website, and finally, turned the microphone over to her.

Skye took a sip of water and smoothed the curtain of hair along her face. She caught Aidan's gaze. He nodded with a wink and she relaxed and began to read. The words she'd practiced rolled off her tongue. At home, she never had her hair in her face when she recorded.

The carefully styled curtain blocked her view from parts of the page. Although armed with an excellent memory, she struggled to resist the urge to tuck her hair behind her ear and rely on her sight.

One page down, three more to go.

Bright sunlight heated the room. Combined with all the people, the temperature rivaled a hot summer day. Her suit jacket and scarf became stifling. The heavy weight of her hair added one more layer to her neck and back. Sweat broke out on her skin but didn't cool her. She flubbed a line—twice.

Another page down.

Halfway into page three, her head swam, sickeningly thick from the heat. One glance up and the room tilted. Dizzy, she gripped the podium with one hand and bit the inside of her bottom lip. The sharp pain brought her back. Fainting would not make a good impression.

The room as too damn warm. She undid her jacket buttons and then clawed the scarf away from her neck. It wasn't enough.

Gulping half the contents of her water bottle did little to help. She had no choice. She eased her right arm out of the jacket. It fell behind her, slipped off her left shoulder and caught at her elbow. Cool air rushed over her skin.

Damon walked toward her. "Are you okay?"

She nodded, and he backed off but stayed close by.

Murmurings drifted from the first row. Raising her gaze, she met sympathetic eyes. Eyes that lowered to her left side. Her upper arm and the inch of chest left bare by her shirt. How much of the scarred skin was visible? How many people could see it? How could she have been so stupid?

Maintaining her death grip on the podium, she pushed through to the last page of the presentation. Her pulse raced, and her hands shook. She managed to tug the jacket back on. The scarf was a mangled mess that required a mirror. Concentration shot, she increased her reading speed. All that mattered was getting out of the spotlight. When the last word faded from the speakers, she turned, quickly shook hands with Damon, and then bee-lined for the doors.

No looking at Aidan.

No returning to her seat.

She had to get away.

CHAPTER FIVE

Amid the murmurs filling the conference room, Aidan pushed to his feet and then raced after Skye. She'd bolted out of the room so fast, he was worried she'd gotten sick. She'd certainly look like she'd been battling nausea up there at the podium and her voice had been strained.

He caught up with her outside the elevators. "Hey. Hold up there. What's wrong?"

She wouldn't turn to face him. "I'm sorry. I have to go."

"Skye?" He gently cupped the back of her arm and stepped closer. After a long moment, she turned toward him.

Staring up at him, brown eyes shining with tears, she seemed so young. "I'm sorry, Aidan."

The tears crushed him. He didn't know how to handle them. "Let's go to my office."

Lips pressed together, she didn't move.

"Come with me." He guided her by the elbow. At last, she went with him and he wished he had a packet of tissues on hand for her tears.

They took the elevator up one floor and then he led her down the hallway to his office. Once inside, he closed the door behind them and gestured to the guest chair by his desk. "Have a seat."

"Thank you." She sat hands in her lap, right over left. "What about the meeting?"

He shrugged. Missing it wasn't too big a deal, not when everyone else was prepped. He shot a quick text to his buddies. "Damon and Hunter can run it without me."

Rather than sit in the chair behind his desk, he sat in the one by her side. He'd had plenty of chats with employees in these chairs, some pretty emotional, but he was ready to tear his own arm off if it would somehow make her feel better. "What happened?"

"They saw."

"Who saw what?"

She blinked at him. "You didn't?"

"Didn't what?" He hoped she wouldn't continue talking in circles before getting to the point.

"You didn't see?" She gazed at him, eyes wide and vulnerable. When he shook his head, she pulled the pink scarf away from her neck.

What was he supposed to… Oh. *Oh.* His focus drew to the skin peeking out of the left side of the scooped edge of her shirt collar. After all he'd seen in the service, he'd know a burn victim anywhere. She pushed the scarf back in place, and he finally got a glimpse of her left hand. No rings, but the same scars covered the back of her hand and disappeared under the sleeve of her jacket.

How much of her skin did they span?

"You must have questions." She pulled on a lock of hair curtaining her face. A nervous habit, he guessed.

He reached out to touch her shoulder, and she shied away. He dropped his hand to his side. "How you feel is more important than my curiosity. If you want to talk about what happened to you, I'm here to listen."

Her face lifted to his, and her expression filled with earnestness and fear. She looked like a recruit on the first day of boot camp. Maybe sharing his story would help her to feel more at ease. "I have scars too. On the inside. As you probably guessed from the video chat, I have PTSD. From when I was in the Army. Loud noises, like a car backfiring or fireworks, are my trigger."

Her face creased in concern and sympathy filled her large brown eyes. "I'm so sorry you have to go through that. You served your country. You're a hero."

He shook his head. "I did my job. That doesn't make me a hero. I knew what I signed up for. But from my time in the Army, I've seen so much bad happen to good people. And from my time working in HR, I've come to understand people. How they think. How they feel. I've had to handle a lot of delicate situations. You can tell me anything. I swear I'm a good listener."

She gave a slight nod and then took a deep breath. "Two years ago, the radio station where I worked held a big beach party with a bonfire. An approaching storm whipped up the wind pretty good. Both the party and the bonfire got out of control. The fire spread to beach blankets and other things. And people. Including me."

Her left hand trembled in her lap. The need to offer comfort was too great. He laid his hand over hers, and she clutched his fingers tight. "I'm so sorry."

The words sounded so empty. They couldn't convey how deeply he meant them.

"Everything changed after that day." Her voice was nearly a whisper. "It's still really difficult for me when people see the scars. To be honest, opening up to people in general since the fire happened has been extremely hard, but I'm trying to work on it."

"I'm happy to hear that because I'd like to get to know you a lot better." If she'd have him.

"If you mean that like I think you do, then there's something I need to show you first." She slipped her hand away from his and took several deep breaths. He was about to tell her not to do anything she wasn't ready to do when her left hand lifted to push her hair away from her face, revealing another scar stretched over her left cheek. Makeup covered the patch of uneven skin.

"Skye." He wanted to touch her. She was trembling, and her pinched expression looked like she was about to face a firing squad.

"Besides my cheek and hand, the scars cover most of the left side of my torso and my left arm. And there are scars on my thighs and butt from where they took skin to do the grafts." Her chin quivered, but she held his gaze.

If the tilt of her head was any indication, the scars had bothered someone else, and that had hurt her. Aidan reached for her hand and tightened his fingers around her palm. Her quiet strength amazed him. "The scars change nothing. I still want to get to know you better."

"I do, too." Hope flickered in her brown eyes a second before the veil of caution set in. "We'll see."

They both were quiet for a long moment. Questions sailed rapid-fire through his brain. Then she spoke again. "I'm sorry if I caused a scene in the meeting."

"It was damn hot in there. If anything, people are going to assume that the heat got to you."

"It did."

He rubbed his thumb over her palm. "Well, there you go then."

"They were staring." Graceful shoulders curled over her chest like she wanted to shrink in on herself. She wrapped her arms around her waist and stared at a spot on the floor.

"Of course, they were. You're beautiful."

Her gaze jumped to his, gaping at him. "But the scars…"

"Still beautiful." He moved closer until their knees bumped together. "Those big brown eyes, that smile, all that wavy blonde hair. Beautiful."

A flush stole over her features, and she smiled even as she shook her head.

"So beautiful, I nearly fell out of my chair the first time I saw you."

"You did not." But her smile grew brighter.

"Did too." He checked the clock on his wall. The presentations portion of the meeting should have ended minutes ago. "Come back with me. This last part is mainly socializing, more like a big party. There's coffee, tea, soda, snacks. Plus, being the voice of the company is similar to a sports star being the face of the franchise. Everyone is going to want to meet you."

"That part sounds a little overwhelming."

"Would it help if I stay by your side?"

She cinched her fingers tightly around his hand. "Yes."

Protective instincts on overdrive, he stood and drew her to her feet. She'd trusted him with something she obviously struggled with, and he was honored. The pain on her face had been heartbreaking. More than anything, he wanted to see her happy.

As soon as they reached the party, he introduced her to Damon and Kira's parents, and then to Kira. Skye was slow to warm up, and now he understood why. But no one could hold out again Kira's friendliness for long. Within minutes, Skye's stiffened posture relaxed as they settled into conversation. He very much liked the idea of them becoming friends.

True to his promise, he stayed by Skye's side as they navigated the room. They spent a long while with the creative team and then met members of sales and IT and the factory workers who made the toys. Skye kept her left side curved into him, as though he was helping her hide the scars from the rest of the world. He didn't want her to feel like she had to hide anywhere, but especially here. Kallis Toys was a family atmosphere. Hopefully, Skye would feel the welcome and eventually relax.

As the party drew to a close, he had her alone, all to himself. "About dinner tonight…"

She stepped closer and peered at him through her curtain of hair. "Is the invitation still open?"

"It is."

"I'd love to go. It'll be my treat, though, to thank you for helping me keep my head earlier."

"Happy to help. It's a pretty head, after all." He grinned and grasped her hand. "Well since dinner's on you," he said with no intentions of letting her pick up the tab, "I hope you're in the mood for Italian. It's close by, and I'm starved."

It was close by, but that wasn't why he'd chosen it. Every table was candle-lit. Romantic. Chances were pretty good, in dim lighting, she'd let her guard down.

CHAPTER SIX

The Italian restaurant smelled amazing, like garlic and tomato sauce, and soft music played with a sultry beat. Candles flickered on each table, casting a soft glow, and sending her heartbeat into a gallop.

Skye stepped into the room ahead of Aidan and her elbow brushed across his torso. Hard, muscled, and solid enough to keep her from backing out of the room. She hid her fear behind a smile, clasped her sweaty palms together, and followed the hostess to a table draped in white linen. The tall, thin white candle flickering in the middle of the table held her attention.

While Aidan took his seat, she blew out the candle, using the movement and noise of pulling in her chair as a distraction. Wisps of smoke danced into the air, coupled with the scent of extinguished flame.

So much for subterfuge. She waved her hand through the fog until it cleared. When Aidan's eyes flicked from hers to the candle, and back, she gave him a weak smile and a shrug. "It must have gone out."

"No worries. Are you all right? You look a little tense."

"I'm fine. You've eaten here before, right? What do you recommend?" She opened her menu and smiled. She'd focus on him, only him, and not on all the tiny fires flickering on all the other tables…

"The ravioli is my favorite. They use a spicy tomato sauce."

"Spicy is good." It was the only kind of heat she liked.

The waiter brought over a plate of crusty bread, and a small bowl of olive oil and spices then explained the house specials. Aidan chose the ravioli and Skye ordered the eggplant lasagna. They both agreed on pinot noir. She slowly relaxed and thought less and less about the candles the more she and Aidan talked.

After their food had been delivered, Aidan slid a piece of his ravioli onto her plate. "You mentioned that you previously worked in radio. Where was that?"

"Miami. I was the DJ for the afternoon drive show." She traded him a slice of the eggplant. "We played a mix of rock and pop. It was a pretty good job. I enjoyed it." And she didn't miss it—not too much. No way could she have stayed.

"How did you end up in Holiday?"

She sipped her wine while she thought of the easiest way to sum up everything without having to rehash all the heartache. "Everything back home was filled with too many reminders of the fire. It was suffocating me. I needed to get away. A clean break. I liked the idea of being somewhere with a long winter—the total opposite of what I had my whole life."

"You grew up there?"

"I did. My family is there. They were amazing to me, but I think they needed a break too."

"I'm sorry for the way it happened, but I'm glad you're here." He reached across the table and covered her left hand with his. She flinched, and he immediately pulled back. "Did I hurt you?"

Heat flaming into her cheeks, she ducked her head. Would she ever react as she used to pre-fire? "It's not smooth like regular skin."

"A journey with detours is more interesting than a smooth ride." Light came into the dark eyes that seemed to see too much and he settled his hand over hers again. His thumb stroked hers as light as a butterfly kiss. "So, what do you do for fun?"

"Fun?" The question had thrown her off. She couldn't drag her attention away from his hand and the gentle caress. "I listen to a lot of music. Read. Watch movies." Hide.

"Anything outdoors?"

Not as much as her life before the fire. "When I lived in Miami, I was a total beach bum. Up here, I like the winter sports—skiing, and ice skating. Other than that, I'm an occasional runner."

His eyes lit with interest, and he leaned forward in his chair, meal forgotten. "You run?"

"Only when it's cold outside." And she could fully bundle up with a hat, scarf, gloves, and layers of clothing.

"If you want company or to add on more seasons, you can join my running group. Damon, Hunter, Kira, and I run on weekday mornings before work. Occasionally, a few guys from the hockey team join us. We do a five-mile loop."

That was tempting. Not just Aidan, but his friends too. Terri would tell her to do it. But the weather was too hot to wear more than a T-shirt and shorts. Could she let them see her that way?

A shadow fell over their table. "How's everything?" The waiter smiled as he spoke. "Oh, the candle…" He pulled a lighter from his apron pocket and reached across the table, carelessly flicking the flame on his way to the candle's wick, less than a foot from Skye's face.

"No." She flung out her arm to stop him and leaped to her feet. The waiter stumbled backward and into a busboy carrying a stack of dirty plates. Dishes and cutlery clattered to the floor.

"I'm so sorry." She jumped up, hands over her mouth, as every eye in the room turned in their direction. Aidan stood, and they both bent to help pick up the mess.

The waiter held up his hand, keeping them away. He exchanged exasperated glances with the busboy. "That's all right, ma'am. Sir. We'll get it. Please sit down."

Skye pushed her hair in front of her shoulder, further shadowing the scars and slunk into her seat. Her cheeks burned, and she couldn't bring herself to meet Aidan's gaze. What was he thinking?

She stared at her plate and listened to the sounds of the clean up. All too soon, they finished and moved away.

"Hey." Voice gentle, Aidan set down his wine glass then his big hand rested over the back of hers. "You okay?"

"Ever since the fire, I really don't like being around any type of open flame. In my mind, any flicker can become an inferno." She shrugged and tried to shake off the embarrassment. "I guess that's silly."

"It's not silly. You went through a scary, life-changing experience and it was only two years ago. Getting comfortable around a flame again is going to take a while. I've been out of the Army for four years, and I'm still adjusting. I may have come back physically intact, but mentally... Well, I don't know if I'll ever stop having flashbacks or if my triggers will ever go away."

From what she understood, PTSD could be like navigating a minefield. She leaned in closer and laced their fingers together and squeezed. "I'm so sorry you have to go through that."

"Thanks. I don't talk about it much, but what I'm trying to say is you never have to apologize for how you're feeling. I understand." This time when his thumb caressed her scarred tissue he wasn't as gentle. Or shy.

A shiver raced along skin she considered dead until Aidan.

"I wish I'd known about how you felt about fire. I never would've suggested we come here."

She squeezed his hand. "It's a great place. Please don't apologize. I need to learn how to handle being around candles or even a gas range oven. I really want to be back to normal again."

"You'll eventually get to a place where you're comfortable. Maybe we can help each other get there." His words were quiet, intimate, and a balm to her soul. All of the other noises—the conversations, the music—faded away.

Help each other? "I'd like that."

He smiled, and that warm light gleamed again in his eyes. "Your voice really is the most soothing one I've ever heard. I've listened to the training modules so many times, I almost have them memorized."

"I'm glad I helped you." Such a small thing, a voice. She was happy hers gave him comfort. "If you want more interesting material, I can record anything you'd like."

"I like hearing your voice in person best. You'll go out with me again, right?"

The waiter approached and stood several feet back from their table, their check in hand. "Will there be anything else tonight?"

Aidan frowned at him. "Nothing else." The frown increased when the waiter made a show of staying as far from Skye as possible as he held out the check. Aidan grabbed the folder. She opened her mouth to protest, but he held up a hand cutting her off. He took one look at the bill and then handed over his credit card.

Less than five minutes later, they stepped out into the warm evening air. Skye tugged on her hair again, smoothing everything in place. "Thank you for dinner. But it was supposed to be my treat."

"Then I guess we'll have to do it again." He stopped at the space between their cars, palming his keys, brows raised in question.

The tug between them was too strong to ignore. She could do this. Looking into his eyes helped her ignore her fears. "Are you free tomorrow?"

"I have a hockey game at six."

"Oh. Well, that's okay. Maybe—"

"Would you want to come?" Earnestness flashed fast across his face. "Damon and Hunter are on my team, and Kira will be there. You can sit with her. The team goes out to a great pub afterward. I think you'd really like it. No asshole waiters, I promise."

A group outing? She'd met his friends, and she'd liked them. She wanted to go. Saying yes shouldn't be this hard.

He stepped closer and laced their fingers together. "It's indoors—air-conditioned—at an ice rink. Not roller hockey out in the heat. You'd be comfortable. I'd really like to see you there."

What's the point in living if you're going to be hidden away? Her sister's words echoed in her head. She couldn't keep hiding. Straightening her shoulders, she stood tall, grasping for confidence. Plus, indoors meant she could comfortably wear a sweater. "I can't wait to see you in action. You know, goalies are my favorite players."

"Yeah? Good to know." The corner of his mouth winged up in a wicked smile. His thumbs traced over the backs of her hands. The sensation wasn't as intense in her left, but she still felt the pressure. He moved even closer and tilted his head down.

Her heart beat wildly in her chest as he raised her trembling hand to his mouth.

His lips grazed the back of her hand—over the scar tissue—and then her knuckles, and then he urged her hand to open and pressed his lips to the center of her palm, shooting the sensation straight to her core.

"Aidan." Her eyes fluttered closed. Leaning into his heat was so tempting, but she couldn't do it. No matter how hard she tried, she couldn't forget about the scars he couldn't see. Scars that could very easily push him away.

He slowly lowered her hands and stepped back. "I'll text you directions to the rink. Or I could pick you up. It's up to you."

Arriving separately would be another layer of separation, and provide an escape if things got to be overwhelming. But together for the drive would give them even more time together, and push her more out of her comfort zone, as her left side would be more exposed to him during the drive. If she could agree to a hockey game, she could agree to the ride. "Going together works. I'll send you my address."

"Drive safe."

"Good night." She dug for her key and slipped inside her car. He gave her another smile and a wave and climbed into his SUV, then sat, watching her. Was he waiting for her to pull away first? The thought made her smile and raised her opinion of him even higher.

She put her car in drive and backed out of the space. Aidan gave her a single nod and then his car began to move. Her stomach tingled at the thought of him caring. She was falling for him. But what would happen when he saw all the scars?

CHAPTER SEVEN

Aidan stood in front of his net and looked around the arena. Anticipation flooded through him. The Blades were about to play the Dragons, the most hated team in the league. But seeing Skye sitting in the first row of the small crowd of the players' family and friends lifted his energy even higher.

He'd picked her up at her house. The decent-sized brick single, lined by pine trees, had a front yard Chance would love. Maybe he'd bring the dog when they got together next. Because there had to be a next time.

She sat beside Kira, hair draped across her face, completely covered up in dark jeans, a white sweater, and that gauzy pale pink scarf she wore at their initial meeting. She laughed at something Kira said, and her whole face lighted with her smile. His heartbeat thudded harder. He wanted to unwrap her, slowly and uncover all her hidden secrets.

"Focused?" Damon stopped by his side and tapped

his pads, with Hunter right behind him. "Ready to kick some Dragon ass?"

"Keep that punk Waverly out of the crease. Last time, he skated into it every chance he got. If he does it again, I'm going to knock him off his skates." Skating into a goalie's sacred space could be a penalty, but Waverly managed to do it and throw in a jab when the ref wasn't looking. The Dragon's resident goon had been as persistent as a pesky fly, taunting Aidan to react. He'd kept his cool—barely.

Hunter turned in a slow circle and eyed the other team. "On it. He's going to have to go through me first. And my fists if he's not careful."

"If you get thrown out of the game again…" Damon shook his head and then laughed. Hunter's level of patience was non-existent when it came to the jerk who'd bothered Kira during a game a few months back. "Then again, it is Waverly, and with his rep, he'll probably get tossed too, so go for it."

The whistle sounded. Damon gave his pads one last tap before skating toward the referee. Aidan dropped his mask into place. It was go time.

Hunter circled in front of him one final time. "Ready to put on a show for Skye?"

Maybe it was silly, but Aidan didn't want to just beat the Dragons tonight. He wanted to mop the floor with them, just to impress Skye. He glanced toward her seat one more time. "I want a shut out."

"Then let's get you one." Hunter grinned and then lined up for the face-off.

The game progressed quickly, and Damon netted two goals in the first ten minutes of play. The Dragons weren't shooting well and were taking stupid penalties. Aidan faced a total of five shots throughout the first and second periods. Easy stops. Easy saves. By the end of the second period, the Blades led three-to-zero, thanks to a goal by Chambers and every Dragons player looked more and more ticked off.

Halfway into the third period, Aidan crouched in net, eyes on Damon and a Dragons player battling for the puck along the boards. Waverly skated by, way too close, his body brushing Aidan's side, blocking his view of the puck.

Aidan nudged him out of the crease. "Watch it, man."

Waverly dove to the ice, arms and legs flopping like a rag doll. He stayed down, motionless while players scrambled around him, chasing the puck. Hunter touched up, and the whistle blew.

The ref pointed at Aidan. "Goalie—two minutes for unsportsmanlike conduct."

Aidan dropped his stick and flipped up his mask. "Are you kidding me? I barely touched him. He should be called for diving."

The ref skated to his side as Damon flew up the ice to join them. "Look, out of the corner of my eye I saw your arm reach toward him, and then I saw him fall."

Aidan glared at the goon slinking his way across the ice. "He was interfering."

"The puck wasn't near either of you." The ref then

turned toward Damon. As team captain, he would determine which of the on-ice players would serve Aidan's penalty for him. "Who's sitting in the box?"

"Hunter will do it." Damon shot a look at their friend. Hunter's mouth opened like he was going to argue. But then he closed it, nodded, and skated toward the penalty box. Damon's decision probably had more to do with Hunter's need to rest his legs than anything else. Hunter always pushed himself too far. Chambers, Hunter's new partner on defense, had lightning-fast speed and would be a better help in killing the penalty.

The ref nodded and headed off toward the face-off circle on Aidan's right. Waverly had stayed on the ice, and the jerk smirked at Aidan and flipped him off behind the ref's back.

Damon leaned in as Aidan slammed his mask in place. "Don't engage. We have ten minutes left. Try some of the Zen breathing shit you're always doing."

"Thanks, man. That's helpful." Frustration forced the words through tight lips. He shook his head and reached for his stick.

Damon waited until he'd stood, then raised a challenge. "If you want that shut out, you'll listen."

"Yeah. Yeah. I know." He breathed deep as Damon lined up in the face-off circle. After another breath, he glanced at Skye. She leaned forward in her seat, hand tugging on the ends of her hair, focused on him. His mood lifted.

He blocked three shots and sent the puck careening around the boards. He'd keep his cool, no matter what.

Led by Damon, his teammates stepped up their play, and they killed off the penalty. *Be one with the puck.* Aidan kept his focus laser-beamed on the rubber biscuit as the minutes ticked by.

Two minutes to go. Then he could be with Skye and knock back a beer with his buddies.

Play stopped when the Dragons took another stupid penalty. A cheap shot to Chambers, checking him head-first into the boards. Then another for cross-checking Damon ten seconds later. At the one-minute mark, the short-handed Dragons pulled their goalie to add on an extra attacker.

Waverly charged up the ice and fired a shot. Aidan dropped low, and the puck crashed into his left pad. He recovered fast and sent the puck down the center of the ice. It sailed into the open net.

Goal!

His first ever. And maybe, his only ever. Goalies in the pros had only scored a handful of times, and a men's rec league wasn't anywhere near the level of professional leagues. At that moment, the little piece of rubber looked better than any trophy.

Aidan's teammates clambered around him, cheering, hugging, and patting him on the back. He met Damon's gaze. "I want that puck."

"Hell yeah. Let's finish off the game with it. Stay solid for the next thirty seconds and you'll have your shut out, too."

He did. His teammates did, too.

The game ended with a final score of four-to-zero.

When they met to celebrate at center ice, he grinned, holding the puck as a scowling Waverly skated away, arguing with his teammates. They'd likely meet again in the playoffs, but until then, he'd savor his goal and the fact that he'd stopped the jerk from scoring one, too.

Skye and Kira waved to him from their seats, and Kira motioned to the spot where they'd meet after the game.

Aidan rushed through his shower and quickly dressed, eager to see Skye. He didn't wait for his buddies and hurried away from the locker room. Hunter always took the longest, needing to stretch out more after the game than the other guys. Either Aidan or Damon usually kept him company while the rest of the team headed over to the pub to grab tables. Today, Damon could do it.

He spied Kira first, lounging against the wall. She hugged him hard. "Congratulations."

Then she stepped aside, and all he saw was Skye. She beamed a grin so bright she probably hadn't realized she'd pushed her hair out of her face. "Great game. I never expected to see a goalie score today. You were amazing out there."

He'd had his best game of the season. His best game in years. Having her there was part of the reason. "I think you brought me some good luck."

Her eyes sparkled, and she shifted a little closer. "If that's the case, maybe I can come to another game?"

He captured her hands in his. "Any time you want."

Damon clapped him on the shoulder. "Are we heading out to celebrate or what?"

Startled, Aidan took a step back. When he was focused on Skye, everything else faded away. That had never happened with anyone before.

"Chambers just sent a text." Damon shoved his phone into his pocket. "The guys are waiting for us at the pub."

"Sure," he said, squeezing Skye's hands and giving her a wink. "Let's go."

During the ride to the pub, she asked question after question about his team, teammates, and their long-standing rivalry with Waverly. He'd love to see her in the stands again, supporting him, cheering him on the way that the other guys' significant others did. And he'd love to have her with him after the games when everyone gathered at the pub to celebrate or commiserate.

When they stepped inside the pub, Skye's hand tensed in his, and she turned her left side more toward his right. Hiding again. The sleeves of her sweater hung low, concealing everything down to her fingertips. He gently squeezed. "They're good guys."

The nerves remained in her gaze, but she smiled and nodded. "Let's go celebrate your win."

They walked up to cheers. Half the guys lifted their beers to him in a toast. Aidan exchanged high-fives and handed Skye a glass of beer before grabbing his own. He made the introductions, and she received another toast as Damon declared her good luck for the team.

Kira had apparently appointed herself head of the *let's welcome Skye committee*, keeping close on Skye's other side. Of course, Aidan shouldn't have expected anything less. He'd told her and Damon and Hunter all about Skye's accident so they'd understand why she might be reserved and also so they could avoid any potential trigger situations. As he chatted with his teammates about the game, he heard the women making plans for the following Saturday for lunch, a stop at the bookstore, and pedicures.

The pub grew more crowded as the night wore on. The more people that squeezed in, the closer Skye drew to him until she was leaning against him. He slid his arm around her, and his fingers played with the strands of hair laying on her shoulder. She fit against him, perfectly. Her fragrance teased up his nose and her curves pressed against his side. He could barely concentrate on the conversations around him. The way her eyes sparkled and her full lips moved hypnotized him.

Skye nodded at Kira and turned to him. "We're going to put in another order for nachos. Be right back."

They'd moved three steps away when a man carrying a wine glass and bottle of beer stumbled into them. The wine glass tipped forward, and its red contents splashed onto Skye's scarf and sweater. Her eyes widened, and her mouth dropped open. She looked down and every limb tensed.

"Sorry," the man slurred. He swayed to the right and then staggered into another table.

Aidan moved fast, but Kira was faster. She grabbed

Skye's elbow. "Let's go to the restroom and try to wash out what we can."

Skye stepped free of Kira's hold. Her hands covered the spreading stain. "Thanks, but I'll go. You stay and enjoy."

"No, no. I'll come and help you cut a path through the crowd." Kira led her away.

Aidan looked at Damon, frustration over the careless drunk firing hot electric through his muscles. "Really? Tonight of all nights?"

Damon shrugged and glanced at the bartender making his way to the drunk. "It happens. At least the glass didn't break. No heading to the ER to have the docs dig glass shards out of anyone's skin."

"That would suck." He kept his gaze trained on the restroom door.

Minutes later, Kira returned. "Skye's upset, of course, but she won't take her sweater off, not that rinsing it in the sink will help all that much with the stain. She said she needed a few minutes by herself. I'd totally forgotten about her scars until we were standing by the sink and she was trying to blot out the stain. It occurred to me then that she might be more comfortable in there alone."

Aidan waited ten more minutes, then set his beer on the table and nudged Damon. "I'll be back."

He made his way to the restroom and knocked on the door. "Skye?"

The door opened. Eyes sad, she held a wet paper towel crumpled in one hand. The red splotch spread across her chest like a bleeding wound. The surrounding area was soaking wet like she'd stuck the sweater under the tap. "I can't get rid of the stain. I don't want to wear this and draw attention all night. I'd like to leave. Please."

Leave? Up until the spill, they'd been having a great time. He wanted his friends to get to know her, and she was sparkling when she let down her guard. No way could she continue to do that with the cold, wet, red reminder on her chest all night. His mind worked for a solution. "I have an idea."

Grasping Skye's hand, he led her through the pub and into the parking lot. The silence seemed loud in the absence of the music and din from the bar. Skye's sandals clicked over the asphalt as they made their way to his car.

"What's your idea?"

He pulled out one of his long-sleeved button-down shirts he'd picked up from the dry cleaner during his lunch break. "Here. Put this on. It's clean."

Her fingertips brushed the navy blue collar. Then she glanced back at the pub with a longing look. "The wine got on my tank top, too. If I wear this, it might seep into your shirt."

She wanted to stay. He pulled the shirt free of the hanger. "I don't care if it does. Seeing you in it will be worth whatever might happen to my shirt."

She held up his shirtsleeve and a little wrinkle formed between her brows. "Seeing me in this? Really?"

"Oh, yeah." He couldn't stop his grin. Nothing looked sexier than a woman's body reshaping a man's plain shirt. Especially post-sex. It would be torture sitting so close and not be able to hold her like he really wanted. "Put it on."

Her eyes darted to his face then the shirt, then back again and she folded her arms across her chest. "Here? Now?"

He glanced around the lot, over the sea of cars, to the deserted road, and the pub's doors. The two patrons who'd been smoking by the entrance had gone back inside. "There's no one out here but us."

Her fingers hesitated on the buttons of her sweater. "That's a lot of skin to show you."

The last thing he wanted to do was make her uncomfortable. "I can turn around."

Color high in her cheeks, she twisted her fingers together in the fabric. "I just... You might not like what you see... But maybe it's better to get that over with now than to wait."

He slung the shirt over his shoulder and grasped her hands. "Your scars don't take anything away from you. They show you were stronger than what tried to take you down."

For a moment, hope shined in her eyes, but then the light dimmed. "That's a nice thought. It really is. But the guy I was dating before the fire couldn't handle how I looked afterward. He dumped me after my last surgery and said he wasn't attracted to me anymore."

"Are you serious?" He couldn't believe someone

could be so callous and cruel, especially after all that Skye had been through.

Her cheeks flushed, and she lowered her gaze. The defeated slump of her shoulders made him boil. "We worked together at the radio station and had dated for five years. He was the program director. He dumped me and then immediately began dating the woman who hosted the morning drive. I couldn't work there after that. Having to deal with him on a daily basis was too hard."

"I'm sorry." His hands tightened as the urge to throttle the guy bore through him. He'd love to tear apart the man who'd hurt her. "I'm not that guy. You know that, right?"

"I do. But still—"

He glided his fingertips up the slope of her neck and cupped her face in his hands. His thumb brushed over the scar on her cheek, then once again to show he didn't care about it. "Trust me."

"I'm trying." She nodded. Teeth sunk into her bottom lip, a red flush still across her cheeks, Skye pulled off her scarf and carefully unbuttoned her sweater. Aidan held his shirt up, ready for her. The white cardigan slipped away, revealing a beige tank top that hugged her curves.

His body hardened. He longed to brush his fingers along her skin, to show her he wasn't going to walk away, but he didn't want to do anything that would upset her or make her shy away. Instead, he waited until she'd slipped her arms into his shirt, and then he drew it over her shoulders and buttoned it up himself. The sleeves hung past her fingertips, and the hem fell to the middle of her thigh.

His blood heated, and he couldn't hold back a growl of approval. "You look way better in it than I ever have. Sexy."

She studied her reflection in the window and rolled the sleeves up enough to free her fingers. "Sexy?"

The wind had tousled her hair. She turned back, and he had a vision of what she'd look like after a long night tangled together. "Oh, yeah."

"Thank you." Skye cupped her hand against his cheek, and she smiled at him in a way that had his blood thrumming. "Ready to go back inside?"

He stepped closer. "Not just yet."

CHAPTER EIGHT

Skye tilted her head back to keep her gaze on Aidan's. The wind pushed her hair away from her face, and she fought the urge to duck her head. The hunger in his gaze stole her breath. All throughout the hockey game, she'd thought about kissing him. All throughout their time at the pub, she'd enjoyed watching him with his friends, and they'd moved closer and closer, leaning into each other. Anticipation built and built until her encounter with the red wine doused it all.

But Aidan had come to the rescue in such a way that she was almost glad the spill had happened. He cared, and it showed.

He rested his hands on her hips and drew her against him. Lowering his head, he hovered his lips inches away her face. Hesitating. Waiting. Skye wet her lips. Her heart pounded at the way his eyes darkened and the concentration on his face. Her left hand grasped his shoulder, and her right hand touched his neck. His warmth seeped into her fingers and the hair brushing his T-shirt collar tickled her skin.

Her heart yearned to feel him. He really wanted her. She hadn't thought that anyone ever would again.

He moved closer and she raised her face and strained closer, eliminating the distance between them. Soft, firm lips met hers and touched sweetly, gently. And then his mouth delved for more. Deeper. Hotter. Hungry. Her lips parted on a sigh, and his tongue traced along her lower lip, sending shivers up her spine.

All her senses were heightened. The sound of crickets chirping. The faint strains of music from the pub. The warm breeze. Aidan's hands sliding along her back. How he kissed her like it was the best thing in the world. And the way his body shifted and brushed and pressed against hers incited more desire than she'd allow herself to feel in a long time.

Skye fisted her hand in his hair, needing and wanting and longing for more. His touch was like a cool drink of water to her starving soul.

His low groan sounded, and he eased back. Thick fingers traced her face. Light touches. Gentle strokes. Like she was something precious. "I've wanted to do that for days."

"Me, too." She laid her hands against his chest. His heartbeat thudded under her palm. The way he smiled at her weakened her knees.

"Tomorrow, if you're free, want to join me for a run?"

"I don't really spend a lot of time outside in the

summer." Turning him down physically hurt and sounded like a lame brush-off, so she elaborated. "To be honest, it's too hot to run in long sleeves and exposing that much skin in workout shorts and a T-shirt kind of freaks me out." Kind of was an understatement. He probably figured that out.

To his credit, he didn't look at her like he thought she was an object of pity. He only nodded and kept up the soft slide of his fingers. "Then how about coming to the park with Chance and me? We go to a place with a lot of trees, lots of shade. It's pretty private. I'll throw in a picnic."

A picnic with him and his dog sounded like a scene in a romantic movie. A scene she very much wanted to be real. "I'd love to."

His grin was the best reward. "I've told him all about you. I'll make sure he's a gentleman."

The pub's door opened, and Damon walked out. He stopped when he saw them. "Just checking to make sure you guys were okay. I see that you are. So I'll, uh, just go back inside now."

He turned to leave, and Aidan called out for him to wait. Then he looked down at Skye and smoothed her hair back in place. "Ready to go in?"

"Definitely." She let her arms fall but his immediately wrapped around her waist.

Damon gave her a sympathetic smile. "That sucks about your shirt. I'm glad you found a spare."

"Yep. Aidan took care of me." She leaned into Aidan as they made their way back to the group.

The next few hours flew by, lots of laughter, and lots of touching—Aidan's hand on her waist, her shoulder, and Skye touching his hand and resting against his side. When he drove her home, he walked her to her door, and they spent a long while saying goodnight.

She fell asleep wearing his shirt and dreaming of a normal life where she didn't have to hide.

The next morning, Skye searched through her closet while talking to Terri over video chat. She set her computer on the bed, and let her sister help veto and approve shirts.

Terri shook her head at the beige canvas top. "I checked the weather where you are, and it's so hot out today. You really should wear something short-sleeved. You're going to roast otherwise."

"I swear you sound like Mom sometimes. I'm wearing shorts, so I should be okay." The knee-length denim shorts completely hid her thighs and fit like a second skin, flexible and comfortable. Perfect for playing with a dog.

"Still." Terri got that stubborn look on her face. "You told me what happened last night. He likes you. He saw your arm and upper chest. He doesn't care about the scars."

"Yeah, but I do. It's not easy to completely change how I've felt since the accident." She pulled out a thin pale gray sweater and one in pastel pink.

"Isn't it time to stop with the boring, blend into the background shades? Adding pops of color to your wardrobe again wouldn't hurt. You used to wear bright stuff all the time."

Skye set the clothes down with a sigh. Her sister's words struck a raw nerve. "Why does it feel like you're picking on me today?"

Terri winced and then shrugged. "I'm trying to help you get back to who you were before the fire. I'm so proud of you for what you're doing. It's not picking on you. It's motivation."

"Fine, Ms. Motivator. I'll try to work on that. But Aidan's going to be here soon, and I can't greet him in a bra and underwear."

"Well, you could, but then I don't think your visit will end with a trip to the park..." Terri wiggled her brows.

Skye burst out laughing. "Okay, you're not helping. At all."

"How about that pink button-down hanging in your closet? You can roll the sleeves up if you get too hot. It would look cute with a white tank top underneath and look good with your shorts. And those flat brown sandals we bought last summer."

"Done." She'd never worn the top outside, worrying it was too sheer. But it would work for today. And she'd add her floppy straw sun hat. "I need to get ready."

"I'd better get a full report in the morning."

"Will do, boss. Thanks." She closed her computer and slipped into the outfit. Aidan's shirt hung by her dresser. She'd have to return it no matter how much she wanted to keep it.

When the doorbell sounded, she checked her makeup one last time, then headed for the door and pulled it open.

Aidan grinned at her behind mirrored sunglasses. His white T-shirt and gray shorts showed off his athletic build. The large Golden Retriever pulling at its leash grabbed her attention. It strained toward her, panting, almost looking like it was smiling.

"Hi." She crouched down and rubbed the soft fur. Chance licked her hand and barked, nudging his head into her shoulder.

"Easy, boy." Aidan pulled him back and helped Skye to her feet. "Sorry, he's excited."

"He's wonderful. Do you want to come in or should we head to the park?"

A loud bark made her jump. Chance sat at attention, tail thumping against the floor. Laughing, she glanced at Aidan. "I guess he knows that word."

"Oh, yeah. There's a list of words I need to spell out instead of say. But he's smart. I'm sure he'll eventually figure those out too."

"Then, let's go." She grabbed her wristlet purse. "Oh, wait. I have your shirt."

"Keep it. I like to think about you wearing it."

Heat flushed into her cheeks. She nodded and locked the door behind her.

The ride to the park didn't take long. The conversation was entertaining with Chance's head bobbing between them from his place in the backseat. Aidan parked beside a gravel trail. He grabbed two bags from the back of his SUV and then let Chance out of the car. "I found this place last year when Damon and I were looking for a new running trail. The trail stops as soon as the road bends so not many people know it's here."

They rounded the curve and strode onto a bed of lush green grass, bordered by tall trees, wildflowers, and a small sliver of the river.

"It's beautiful. So peaceful."

"It's one of my favorite places." He set down the bags and pulled out a tennis ball. "Want to throw it to him?"

"Sure." Chance danced around her legs, eager for the ball. She hefted it toward the trees, away from the water, and the dog darted after it.

"No worries if you get it in the water. Chance usually finds himself in there once or twice a trip. It's not deep, and the current is mild." Aidan spread out a red blanket underneath a tree. "Is this enough shade for you?"

"It's perfect." She tugged on the end of her shirt-sleeve. Maybe she could roll up the sleeves just a little. Chance bounded back and dropped the ball at her feet. She rubbed his head and tossed it again.

They played fetch for a while. Then Aidan brought out the Frisbee. They threw the neon yellow disc back and forth with Chance jumping up for it every time. Skye laughed hard at his antics and loved seeing the obvious affection Aidan had for his furry friend.

Sweat slid down her back. She rolled her sleeves to her elbows and pushed her hair off her neck, wishing for a hair tie, but she never wore her hair up in public. Ever.

Aidan tossed the Frisbee into the bag. "What to have lunch? Chance needs a water break, and I could use one, too."

They settled onto the blanket. He filled Chance's water and food bowls first, then pulled out sandwiches and cold sodas. "Turkey with bacon on whole-wheat? Or roast beef on rye?"

"Turkey, please." She accepted the sandwich and twisted open the soda. As they ate, the gurgling of the river, the chirping of the birds, the soft breeze, and the smell of the grass relaxed her. "This really is a great spot."

"It's sort of secret. Maybe I should have blindfolded you before bringing you here." He winked and tossed his sandwich wrapper into the bag. "I might have brownies for dessert."

"You shouldn't tease about chocolate."

"Sorry. I definitely have brownies for dessert. And a t-r-e-a-t for Chance."

"I had a feeling he'd know that word for sure."

Aidan glanced at his dog and shook his head. "You should see him at Halloween. Every time some kid rings the doorbell and says 'trick or you-know-what' he goes nuts."

She giggled, nearly choking on her mouthful of soda. "Oh my goodness. I'd never have even thought of that."

"I finally figured out last year to put him in my bedroom with a movie playing." He handed her the brownie. Then he pulled out a bone-shaped biscuit for the dog. Chance pounced on Aidan, then lay down in the grass gnawing on his treat. Aidan wiped his hands and picked up his own brownie. He laid on his side with his head close to Skye. She shimmied down beside him, and they finished eating and then watched the clouds rolling by.

"This really is peaceful. Thanks for asking me to come today."

He rolled until he faced her. "Want to do it again next Sunday?"

"Uh, sure." She couldn't believe how easy it was to be with him. How he seemed to be content to move at her pace.

He cupped her cheek with his hand and then brought his lips to hers. He tasted like chocolate. Their tongues teased together, bodies shifting closer as the kiss went on. His hand left her cheek and traveled down her arm in a slow stroke. She stiffened for a moment, wondering if he could feel that the skin was different and if that would break the mood, but then he changed the angle of the kiss and took it deeper, and the only thing that mattered was how good she felt in his embrace.

CHAPTER NINE

Skye strolled into Kallis Toy Factory, ready for her full day of meetings with Sales and Marketing and the creative team. She'd spent the last two days with Kallis employees—lunch and shopping for hours with Kira on Saturday, and a second trip to the park with Aidan and Chance on Sunday that had ended in dinner at his place. He'd made tacos, and then they'd sat together watching a movie while Chance napped on the floor. She was falling for the dog and his master.

Aidan waited for her by the reception desk, much like the first time she'd visited Kallis. When he saw her, his face lit with a smile. He strode to her, wearing a navy suit and pale blue tie. Rather than extending his hand, he bent and kissed her—a light, quick brush of lips that she still felt all the way to her toes. And then he led her to the bank of elevators. "Sleep okay last night?"

"The movie wasn't too scary, so yeah. But I still checked behind my shower curtain after I got home."

They stepped into the empty elevator car. "You could have called me. I wouldn't have minded coming over."

"And checking out my shower?"

"Sure. I'd check under the bed too." He leaned in and kissed her again. "Maybe inside the sheets."

Laughing, she rested her hands on his shoulders. "I think I'd notice if someone were hiding in my bed, under my comforter."

"Can't be too careful. I'd suggest we start our search there and see what happens."

She let that image linger for a moment in her mind. It wasn't the first time she'd imagined it. "I think I know what would happen."

"Me, too." His voice deepened, and he ran his finger along the scalloped collar of her dress. The touch sent a delicious shiver down her spine. Each time they got together, the physical pull for more was harder and harder to resist. But as comfortable as she was with him touching her face or her hand or her arm, she still wasn't ready for him to see the rest of her scars.

The car stopped, and the doors opened with a soft ping. He drew her down the hall to the break room. "Coffee first."

Three coffee makers sat on a counter. The decaf was closest to her. She filled a cup and passed it to Aidan then laughed as he handed her a cup of regular brew. She added cream and sugar, the light and sweet a contrast to Aidan's black, nothing added, preference.

He tucked her hair behind her right ear. "I think

Chance was looking for you this morning. He kept going into the living room and staring at the couch."

The image made her smile. "Are you sure he doesn't have a toy trapped under it?"

"I checked. Maybe you'll come to dinner tonight? He'd like that. I'd like it, too."

"I can't. I have some projects to record that are due tomorrow. It's going to be a pretty busy week for me." She hated the idea of not seeing him. "Maybe Friday night?"

"Definitely Friday night." He bent until their foreheads touched. Eyes closed, she breathed him in.

Male voices, touched with laughter, drew closer, and then Hunter and Damon came into the room. Damon set a box of bagels and muffins on the counter. "Morning, Skye. Aidan."

Hunter greeted them and then pulled out his phone and held it out to Aidan. "Check it out. The site reservation confirmation finally came through this morning."

Aidan exchanged a high-five with his friend. "The permit for Chance did, too."

"Awesome. Can't wait, bud." Damon snagged a muffin and filled a cup with coffee. "We should all do a final gear check this week and make a food list."

"Kira and I did a check yesterday. Something chewed through my tent, but hers is fine, so we'll use that. We're all set on everything else." Hunter grabbed a bagel and tilted the box toward Skye.

She chose a chocolate chip muffin and glanced from one man to the next, brows raised in question.

Aidan met her gaze. And for the first time since she'd met him, he looked embarrassed. "We're going camping."

She'd been with both Kira and Aidan for hours and hours over the weekend, but neither had mentioned camping to her. She pasted on a polite smile and tried not to let the awkwardness of feeling left out bother her. "That's nice."

Kira strode in, heels clicking on the floor. "Morning, all. Skye, I love that dress." She slipped her arm around Hunter's waist and selected a muffin. "I'm starving. Today's run was brutal. Guys, make sure you hydrate."

The reminder of the morning run group stung. The activity she should be doing, would be doing, if she wasn't such a coward. Her fears only further isolated her from a group of people she genuinely liked and wanted to spend time with and an activity she enjoyed doing. Skye picked a chip out of her muffin, frustrated and annoyed that returning to normal seemed so impossible.

Kira filled a coffee cup and added a healthy dose of peppermint creamer. "Skye, if you're ready, my team is all set for our meeting."

"Sure." She gripped her breakfast and glanced at Aidan. "I guess I'll see you later."

He nodded and took a step toward her, but she turned away and followed Kira from the room.

She told Kira's team how impressed she was with their writing and wording of the sales scripts, then added in suggestions while they brainstormed on new ideas. Occasionally, a client would request help with script writing. She loved working the creative part of her brain.

After the meeting, she sat with Kira, sharing lunch in her office. Their shopping day had given her a taste of friendship that she hadn't had since moving away from her friends in Miami. Being in stores among crowds of people, she'd still been conscious of whether her hair and scarf and sweater were in place, but Kira's easy laugh and the animated conversation had distracted her from dwelling on it. For the first time in years, she'd relaxed while shopping. And she had Kira to thank.

Skye stabbed a forkful of penne pasta, cherry tomatoes, and feta cheese. Kira treated her with nothing but kindness. She shouldn't worry too much about a camping trip that was probably planned well before she came into Aidan's life. "Thanks again for lunch. I've never had Greek pasta salad before."

Kira speared an olive from her identical dish. "It's so good, right? I'm lucky this place delivers. Everything on their menu is great. The guys and I all have different favorites. When we have dinner with my parents, we end up with six main dishes and six sides. Way too much food. You'll have to come next time. We do family dinner every few weeks."

That sounded fantastic, but... "I wouldn't want to intrude on a family thing."

Kira set her fork aside. "It's my parents, Damon, Hunter, Aidan, and me. Chance comes too. You're more than welcome."

"Thanks. I'd like that." Family dinners, home

cooked meals, were something she missed. No matter how many times she made a recipe, it never turned out quite as good as when her mom made it.

"Good. The next one is the night before we go camping. Dinner is always at six-thirty. I'll text you directions, but I imagine you'll come with Aidan."

"He might be too busy getting ready for the trip." Maybe she shouldn't go. After all, these were Aidan's friends and Aidan's tradition. She didn't want it to seem like she was forcing herself into too many areas of his life.

Kira rolled her eyes. "Trust me, the guys are all set. They're excited. It's all they've been talking about during our runs for weeks. We go camping every fourth of July."

All they'd been talking about, but he'd never mentioned it. Skye speared a tomato. "That's a fun tradition."

"Fireworks aren't good for Aidan. Since he's been here with us, we go to a campground that doesn't allow them."

The hurt faded under the reason for the trip. "It's really sweet that you guys do this for him."

Kira smiled and lifted her shoulders. "The guys are tight. They function as a unit, and they've been through a lot together. Aidan is like family to me. And Hunter's going to be family soon." She smiled down at her engagement ring.

Skye nodded. Loneliness was an acute pain in her chest. What if she never got to a comfortable place where she could fully share herself with Aidan? How long until he grew frustrated and moved on?

Kira picked up her fork and scooped up a bite of the salad. "Have you ever gone camping?"

She pulled her sweater sleeve over her left hand, hiding the scar. "Never. My family was always more of the beach type."

"Would you want to try it?"

Skye braced against the flush of anticipation in her chest. From Kira's tone, she thought she knew what was coming next. "Sure. Someday."

"Do you have plans for the holiday?"

"Nothing definite." The day would be spent either reading one of the new novels she'd purchased during their shopping trip or watching a few movies. But if Kira asked her along to camping, she couldn't agree. Not with the way Aidan had looked that morning. She needed to change the subject. "Have you and Hunter made any wedding plans? Did you start shopping for your dress?"

Kira's face broke into the biggest smile. She was off and running, and for the next half hour, Skye heard all about the venue selection and Kira's experiences wedding dress shopping with her mother, aunts, and grandmothers.

The pang of loneliness increased. Maybe she'd call Terri when she got home. Then again, maybe not. She wasn't up for more motivation. All she wanted was a sympathetic ear to listen. A hug would be nice too. But thanks to her own doing, she was all alone.

CHAPTER TEN

Aidan punched the return key and sent off the new hire's health insurance forms. With the understaffed Sales department now back to a full team, he could finally shift more of his attention to other projects that had been pushed aside. He looked up at the quick rap on his door.

Kira strode in and stopped in front of his desk, hands on her hips. "You have to invite Skye to come with us."

He shook his head in an attempt to clear it. "What?"

"She's so lonely, Aidan." She sank into one of his guest chairs. "I can tell. She got a longing look on her face when we were all talking about the trip. You guys are dating, we all like her, so I think we should ask her to come."

"I'd thought about asking her, but the nightly campfire might be too much for her. I don't want to do anything to hurt her or make her remember something she doesn't want to relive."

"We don't have to have a fire."

"Even if we don't, most of the other campers will." He pushed away from his desk. "Flickering candles on other tables at a restaurant freaked her out. Who knows how she'd react to campfires all around her."

The hurt look on Skye's face had bothered him all day. He hadn't been trying to deliberately hide the trip from her. Hell, the fact that he had to go away, that his problem pulled his friends away from enjoying normal festivities, annoyed him like crazy. "Maybe I should go alone this year."

Kira's mouth dropped open. "Why?"

Before he could even try to formulate his thoughts, another knock sounded, and Damon and Hunter walked in. Damon glanced around the room. "Where's Skye?"

"She's recording some voiceovers with the creative team until three-thirty." Kira stood and faced her brother. "Aidan thinks he should go camping alone."

His best friends looked at him with raised brows. Damon spoke first. "Something going on?"

Aidan shoved his hand through his hair, feeling stupid. "Look, you guys. You don't have to go."

"Why wouldn't we go?" Damon shot back. "I need to get away."

"We've been planning this for weeks." Hunter lowered himself into the second guest chair, arm raised for Kira to fit in against his side. "What's wrong?"

"My problem is my problem. I should deal with it on my own, not bother you all with it."

Damon sat on the edge of Aidan's desk. "Since when do we not bother each other?"

Kira nodded, and her chin jutted out in the stubborn expression she shared with her brother. "Aidan, we love you. You have done and would do anything for us. Let us be there for you."

He appreciated hearing that and seeing that they all meant it. But still…

Damon tilted his head, brows narrowed, studying Aidan. "Is this about Skye? Do you want to go with her instead?"

"No. I'd like her to come with us, but I don't know how she'd be around the campfires."

"So tell her about them. Explain what it's like." As Hunter spoke, he rubbed his hand up and down Kira's back. "Let her know we'll all be there. There will be plenty of us to make sure the fire is put out."

"Ask her." Kira chimed in. "If she says no, then fine. But ask."

"I will." Having Skye along would be perfect. With her by his side, he'd be able to fully relax.

Damon pulled out his phone and opened up his notepad app. "Good. Now that's settled, we need to talk food for the trip. Who's bringing what?"

Part of the weight Aidan had carried around lifted. They did help each other. Always had. This wouldn't be any different, and he couldn't imagine going without them.

For the next half hour, he thought about what he'd

say to Skye as his friends debated and assigned different foods.

At three-thirty, he went in search of Skye. He stopped in the creative department but was told the creative director had left just minutes earlier to walk her down to the building's entrance. He needed to talk to her before she left. He had to clear the air. He ran for the elevator, caught an open one, and pressed the button for the lobby.

He arrived to see the director coming back into the building. "Where's Skye?"

"Probably still walking across the parking lot."

"Thanks." He jogged past. When he opened the door, the heat slammed into him. Squinting against the harsh sunlight, he spotted her at the back of the parking lot. He ran faster. "Skye!"

She turned, eyes hidden by large, dark frames. Her muscles seemed to stiffen, and her smile didn't form.

He stopped in front of her. Her stance didn't alter and in the absence of her smile, he realized how much he depended on seeing it light up the world around her. "You weren't going to leave without saying goodbye, were you?"

"I figured you were busy. And I need to get home."

"Right. Those voice jobs." He stepped closer but didn't risk touching her. "Before you go. I wanted to ask, would you want to come camping with us? We're leaving late morning on July Fourth, and will be gone for two nights. Two weeks' notice isn't a lot, but I hope you'll come."

She crossed her arms over her chest. "Are you asking for yourself or for Kira? She hinted at inviting me earlier, but I saw your expression this morning. Don't worry, I'm not going to infringe. Just because we've been hanging out doesn't mean I have to go to or expect to be invited to everything you do." Her lenses weren't dark enough to fully conceal her eyes or the hurt in them.

That hurt demanded action and an explanation. His own temper threatening to simmer, he placed his hands on her shoulders. In the span of a day, things had spiraled out of control. "Hold on there. One, we're doing more than just hanging out. Two, I didn't bring up the camping because I was a little embarrassed about needing to go away. And three, I wanted you there but didn't know how you'd be around campfires. I don't want to send you back to a dark place."

Her eyes widened, and her mouth worked open and close for a moment. "Oh."

"Yeah. Oh." Under his hands, the tension in her shoulders eased. He kneaded them anyway. "I can promise that between the five of us, we'll make sure the campfire is completely put out. There will be other campfires, but most of the campers we see there are experienced. So what do you say? Will you come?"

"I… Sure. I'd like that. Thank you." A real smile lit her features, but something still seemed to hold her back.

He pulled until she stepped forward and lined up

against him. "I'll let you go. I know you're busy. But I'm glad you're coming. See you Friday, right?"

She nodded and kissed him. Something in her kiss was off too. He lifted his head. "What's wrong?"

"I just… It was a bit of a rough day." She tugged on the ends of her hair until it curtained her face. He'd thought they were past that.

"Remember when I said I was a good listener? That's still true." Whatever was wrong, he wanted to fix it. He slipped his arms around her back and drew her against his chest. "Are you sure I can't stop by and bring dinner tonight? You have to eat, right? I won't stay long. Just enough to make sure you eat, and for Chance to say hello."

Her arms came around him then, almost desperately tight. Relief and comfort washed through him. He'd needed to receive the hug as much as he'd needed to give it. "I might only have time to take a twenty-minute break."

"We'll take that deal." He knew Skye really enjoyed his dog. Chance had helped him so much, maybe he could help her too. Plus, after the day he'd had, he needed to see her again, not only to make sure she was okay but for himself too.

He was navigating the relationship by flying blind. Hopefully, he wouldn't crash and burn.

Friday night hadn't arrived fast enough. Aidan picked up Skye after work. Kira had made plans for them all to try a new bar on the other side of town. He double-checked the bar's address and pulled onto the road. "Busy week for me. Did you get through all of your projects?"

Skye nodded and leaned her head back on the seat. "I did. And now I can relax all weekend."

"Good. Think you can fit an over-excited Golden Retriever and me into your plans? I'm beginning to think Chance likes you more than he likes me."

"No way. You're his favorite. I'm just new."

He had a feeling there was more to it than that. Chance had worked his canine magic on Monday night. He'd crawled right onto Skye's lap and let her pet him for the full half hour they'd been at her house. She had opened her door looking like she'd lost her best friend, but when they'd left, she was back to her happy self. He liked to think he'd helped there too.

She twisted toward him. "I have some questions about camping."

"Ask away." He glanced at the traffic in his rear view mirror and changed lanes.

"What do I need?"

"You won't need to buy anything. We have tents, and we'll bring all the supplies."

"I'll need some direction on what to pack."

"Shorts. T-shirts. You can get by with sneakers, so you don't need to buy hiking boots. We'll stick to easy trails if we do any hiking. You might want a few thin, long-sleeved shirts, and probably a sun hat. Sunscreen. There are showers and regular bathrooms. We're not completely roughing it."

"What about a sleeping bag?"

He placed his hand on her knee. "You can share mine."

Her thigh muscles jumped and then her fingers covered his hand. "Sleeping bags are made for one person. Won't that be a little tight?"

He wouldn't mind extremely close quarters at all. "Not really. I have a large one. It's actually made for two people. Chance likes to sleep in it sometimes."

"So I'll be kicking my favorite dog out of his bed?"

He couldn't hold back his chuckle. "Don't worry. I'll bring his blanket for him."

"Maybe I'll buy him a present. A new toy so he doesn't feel left out."

"And that's why you're his favorite person." He pulled into a parking space and cut the engine. "Are you sure you're going to be okay with the campfires?"

Her brow wrinkled, and she pressed her lips together for a moment, but then she nodded. "I really want to get comfortable with it again. And it's not going to be like a big bonfire, right?"

"Right. Small campfires. And the closest fire station is less than half a mile outside the campground."

"Then I think I'll be okay. I need to try. And you'll be there with me." She laced their fingers together and brought his hand up to rub against her cheek.

He closed his eyes when she kissed his knuckles.

He'd rather be at home with her, unwinding with a beer, than out at a place that advertised all of their drinks in neon colors, and decorated with glow sticks. "Ready to try this place? I hope it's not a dive."

She released his hand and grabbed her wristlet bag. "It just opened so it could be amazing or awful. Let's hope for amazing."

Kira met them at the entrance. "Come on. Drinks and our table are in the back."

The walls were black, and the only light came from blacklight-painted murals decorating the walls and glow in the dark stars dotting the ceiling. Aidan greeted Hunter and looked around for Damon. His friend stood at the bar, downing a shot. Aidan figured he might need one too, to deal with all the day-glow colors screaming from the walls. He shook his head at the decor and turned to Kira. "How did you find this place?"

"One of the guys in IT mentioned it to Hunter." Kira pulled Skye toward the dance floor. "Come on. Let's dance."

A wistful expression crossed her face. "I don't know…"

The floor was as shadowed as the rest of the place. Aidan moved to take Skye's hand, and Kira grabbed his wrist too. "You two go ahead. I'm going to grab Hunter."

Hunter stayed on his barstool, drink in hand. "Good luck with that."

Skye laughed as Kira pushed them both out onto the

dance floor and then returned to Hunter to playfully tug on his arm. "She's feisty."

"She had to be, growing up with Damon." Aidan wrapped his hand around Skye's waist and pulled her against him. He wasn't the best dancer, and he didn't care if the beat was slow or fast, if they were going to dance, he wanted to feel her lined up with his body, moving right along with him.

They danced, slow, sexy, moving freely in the darkened space. Skye's hands traced his arms, his chest, his stomach. Bold moves, making him want, making him need. He let his fingers smooth over her curves. As he learned her shape and she shifted with him in time to the music, he hardened, his body throbbing to the beat of his heart.

Her breath caught. Then her leg came up and rubbed against the back of his thigh, clamping him close. He groaned deep in his throat and laved her neck with his tongue.

He pulled her closer, his hands sliding along her back until they rested at the curve of her hips, then dipped lower. Her arms wound around his neck, and her breasts pressed against his chest, teasing, tempting him to take more. Each kiss was like downing another shot of an intoxicating aphrodisiac. Blood rushed to his head. Hidden in the shadows, their bodies brushed soft and slow and then rougher and faster, sparking arousal and pleasure higher and higher.

He couldn't touch enough, but he needed to reign it

in before he was too far gone to think clearly and ended up taking her on the dance floor.

Easing back, he took a second to clear his head. Then he adjusted his shirt and helped her smooth her own—the fabric wrinkled by his hands. "Even with what just happened, you know there's no pressure with us sharing the tent or sleeping bag, right?"

"Yes." Her breathless voice danced along his skin.

He longed to hear that word when he was buried deep inside of her, wrapped in her heat and scent, where nothing else existed except the two of them. But he'd wait until she was ready, however long it took.

CHAPTER ELEVEN

Skye squinted against the sunlight streaming through the windshield of Aidan's SUV. The campground was hidden in a state park and surrounded by mountains in the distance, rugged hills, trees everywhere, and small waterfalls.

"It's beautiful."

"Yeah. Damon found this place after we learned that fireworks don't agree with me." His sunglasses hid his expression. Skye reached over and squeezed his knee, offering support. Chance leaned his head forward from the backseat and laid it on Aidan's shoulder.

They followed behind Damon's car where she could see Hunter and Kira looking through the other half of the gear for something. When Damon hit a rut in the graveled road, both their heads bounced off the interior roof. She cringed a little then turned her attention to the scenery once more. They were passing rows of small, wooden cabins.

Skye twisted toward Aidan. "Wait. There are actual cabins here, but we're sleeping in tents?"

He grinned and slowed to a stop at their camp site, then tugged on the brim of her sun hat. "Tents are fun."

She'd reserve judgment on that. Her experience with tents was limited to the blanket forts she and Terri had built as kids.

Helping with the unloading of the vehicles, she thought they'd packed a lot for a two-day stay. Three tents, sleeping bags, three large coolers, a few mesh chairs, a small grill, two bags filled with food, and a bag with flashlights and other necessities.

They set up the tents in a triangle, with each on an opposite side of their campsite. A yellow and gray dome tent for Aidan and Skye. Red and blue for Damon. And Hunter and Kira had black and green. Space would ensure some privacy.

Aidan set their gear in the tent and grabbed her hand. "Come on. Let's take a walk before dinner."

They wandered away from the others, and he took her on a tour of the campground. He pointed out the showers and restrooms, the hiking trails he preferred, and a crystal clear lake that Chance loved. They passed other campers, including a group of college-age kids with several wearing the colors and logo of the local university. They were playing with a Frisbee in front of a small cluster of cabins. Alcohol was flowing freely, and they had cases and cases of it.

Aidan kept a tight grip on Chance's leash. "No,

buddy, they aren't here to play with you. Let's go back and you can play with the gift Skye gave you."

Skye rubbed the dog's head. "Such a good boy. I hope he likes it."

"You gave him a chew toy that dispenses treats. It's pretty safe to say he'll love it forever." He nudged her shoulder and, when he smiled at her with a hint of smolder in his eyes, her stomach fluttered.

They returned to the site. Damon pointed to a small propane grill. "The burgers are almost ready."

Kira and Hunter were setting out containers of watermelon and blueberries, potato chips, and then buns, sodas, and beers.

Skye's focus scanned past the food and landed on the fire pit and the flames licking the logs.

She stopped cold in her tracks. Despite all of Aidan's reassurances and her growing attraction to him, her stomach lurched. Heart beating like a humming bird's, her limbs fired with energy to flee. Panic strangling her throat, she took a step back and banged into Aidan.

"Whoa there." He turned her by the shoulders. "You okay?"

"I'm sorry," she stammered the apology. Her gut twisted, not wanting to ruin his holiday, but her instincts pulled harder. "I... I can't do this. I need to leave. Now."

She wrenched from his hold and, with her gaze on the fire, she backed up another step. Then another, and tugged her sweater tighter around her like a shield.

Then Aidan's arms came around her, and he hugged her against his chest. "The fire is contained. Look at it. And we're all ready to put it out when the time comes. If you want us to put it out now, we can. But I guarantee you're going to see, smell, and hear other campers' fires tonight." His lips brushed her ear, his tone soft and gentle. "But I don't want you to be upset or scared. I can drive you back home. No problem and no hard feelings. I promise."

Damon set down a plate of cooked burgers and regarded her with sympathetic eyes. "We have plenty of water, enough to put out five fires. We know what we're doing, we're not going to leave it unattended, we're all just going to sit right here and watch it."

Hunter and Kira both voiced their agreement. Skye sucked in one deep breath, then another. She he had said she wanted to be more comfortable with fire. Chickening out now wouldn't be very brave. "Okay. Okay, I can try to do this. I want to do it."

"You're doing great. And if you change your mind, then I'll take you home." Aidan's low voice sent a warm rush over her skin. "Come on. We'll sit by the water."

They settled onto two of the mesh chairs, closest to the water and farthest from the flames. The low to the ground seats reclined a bit and gave her a great view of the sky. She continued with the deep breaths and kept her gaze on the fire. Chance settled in front of her, laying on her feet while he gnawed at his new kibble-filled toy.

Throughout the meal, Aidan kept a connection of his hand on her back or her knee or his arm around her. She ate the burger and drank her beer and relaxed degree by degree.

Sunset was beautiful, the setting sky awash in colors of an artist's palette, until they drifted away over the horizon as dusk took over. Then the star winked out of the growing black, one by one. Peaceful. Quiet. Serene. Other campers started fires, but she tried not to think about them too much. Aidan and his friends went out of their way to keep her at ease. She really enjoyed being with the group, and Aidan most of all.

Hunter handed out long roasting forks. "Ready for toasted marshmallows?"

"Sure." Resolved to roast her own, she grabbed hold of the fork. She wouldn't make Aidan or anyone else do it. But as she edged closer, nerves stirred and her muscles resisted moving closer to the flames. Annoyance flashed along with the fear and she placed a marshmallow on the fork then held it over the fire, ready to drop the utensil if needed. Watching the sugars crisp and burn was hypnotizing. When she pulled it back, Aidan helped her blow on it to cool it down.

"Together." His smile was wicked. He pointed to one side of the marshmallow. "Yours." Then the other. "Mine." He inclined his head and waited for Skye to lean forward.

She nibbled on the outer shell and stilled as Aidan bit into the side of the treat. His lips brushed hers and his tongue swept in for a taste. In the intimacy of sharing the treat that way, she forgot about their audience until Kira whispered, "Aren't they cute?"

Laughing with Aidan, she pulled back.

Maybe this whole camping thing was a pretty brilliant idea after all.

Aidan stared at the fire pit. Flames licked and curled, devouring the logs. Too bad he couldn't erase his demons as easily.

Beside him, Skye laughed at something Kira said. She'd relaxed against him, soft curves temptingly close. He kept one arm around her and swallowed the rest of his beer. He was so glad she'd come. She fit in well with his friends, like a missing puzzle piece. Hunter and Damon teased her as much as Damon teased Kira.

He leaned over her to chuck his empty beer bottle in the trash and steal a kiss on the way back.

Boom.

The sound tore through the air. It seemed the starry sky shuddered from the explosion.

Pop. Pop. Pop. Pop. Pop.

He grabbed Skye, tucked, and rolled them to the ground, covering her body with his own. Frozen against Skye, Aidan's muscles seized, paralyzing him while memories ripped his heart open. The explosions continued in a barrage of pops and bangs. He bowed tighter around her. He'd protect her. Always.

"Aidan. Aidan." Her voice teased his ear, calling him from a faraway tunnel. She shifted under him and her fingers dug into his shoulders. "Aidan. Breathe. Focus."

He breathed in the scent of lavender.

Skye.

Skye wasn't a soldier.

Blades of grass tickled his cheek.

Grass.

They weren't on a battlefield.

The pops faded. Crickets chirped. And fire crackled. The real world came back to life.

"Aidan?" Skye lifted a hand to his face. Warm fingers caressed his brow. Her brown eyes filled with sympathy and understanding. "You're okay. We're all okay. Just breathe for me."

Sweat chilled his skin. He focused on those eyes and drew in long, slow breaths as she continued to talk and touch. Finally, his heart rate returned to normal.

"Good. Good." She shifted against him and his brain registered their position. He had to be crushing her.

He rolled to his side, rose, then carefully hauled her to her feet. "Shit. I'm so sorry. Are you okay?"

"Of course." Her hand latched around his, and she squeezed tight.

The rest of his surroundings came into focus. Dark woods, orange flames, and the concerned faces of his friends. Anger bolted him forward—away from Skye, away from everyone. What the hell had happened?

Fireworks—he answered his own question.

Damn it.

Rage at whoever had set them off consumed him until his blood boiled.

Chance rubbed against his leg, a velvet ear slid beneath his fingertips. He needed to calm the hell down, to get a grip on himself before he lost control of his temper completely. Sucking down another deep breath, he grabbed hold of Chance's leash and walked toward the tree line, ignoring his friends' calls.

Shit. Shit. Shit.

Deep breath in. Count to four. Let it out. Count to eight. Over and over again.

Fist clenched, he leaned against a tree, head resting on his forearm, fighting for that sense of calm. So much for a safe haven. Anger waged war with frustration. His muscles burned with the urge to search out the idiots who'd disregarded the rules and make them pay. Who knew—maybe they had more and weren't yet finished with their celebrating. The notion of a possible third loss of control in front of Skye was enough to make him want to pack up and head for home. But he couldn't do that to his friends.

Chance whimpered and nudged his leg, then let out two short barks. Aidan lifted his head. Skye walked toward him, pace hurried, biting her lip.

"Hey." She stopped by his side, and her hand stroked up and down his back.

He closed his eyes and concentrated on her touch, and then on her words. She talked about the trip and how much fun she'd had hiking and roasting marshmal-lows, how much she enjoyed his friends.

Slowly, he let go of the tree, and then turned and wrapped his arms around Skye. He buried his face in her neck, breathed in her scent, and held on tight.

He needed, not just wanted, but needed her. With her, the anger, the frustration, and the embarrassment faded.

The gentle strokes on his back continued then rose higher to his neck and hair. Every touch soothed and centered him.

For a long moment, they held each other while fire-flies glowed against a starry sky.

Skye's strokes slowed to a stop. She drew back and laid her hand on his cheek. "Are you okay?"

He threaded his fingers in her hair and bent to kiss her, taking comfort in her tenderness. "Let's go back. Get some sleep."

Hand in hand, they walked back to the site. Damon and Hunter were pouring water over the fire pit while Kira finished cleaning up the remnants of their snacks. Damon set the water jug aside and patted Aidan's shoul-der. "We walked around but didn't see who had the fire-works. Sorry, bud. You okay?"

With a nod, he shoved his hands in his pockets. "Yeah. Sorry. So much for no episodes."

"Not your fault, man." Hunter picked up the rocks forming the ring, making sure they were cool to the touch. He doused the pit then motioned for Skye to come closer. "The fire is completely extinguished. Let me show you."

He scraped through the ashes with a stick, and Damon poured more water. "See? No hissing, no smoke, and no embers. Everything is cool."

"Thanks, guys." She accepted the stick from Hunter and sifted through the pit too—calm, focused, and no hint of her earlier fear. Aidan watched her while pride pushed through his other emotions. She'd held herself together. She was way stronger than she believed.

"Aidan, here." Kira held out her cupped hand. "Ear plugs. Just in case those idiots try setting off any more."

He pocketed the foam plugs. They wouldn't erase the sounds but would hopefully muffle them enough that he wouldn't have another episode. "You think of everything."

"I take care of my family." She hugged him. "If you need anything tonight, just yell. I know you have Skye, but we're all here for you too."

Together, they joined the group by the fire pit. His friends laughed and joked like everything was normal. He inhaled another deep breath and gave silent thanks to the universe for placing these people in his life.

Minutes later, he took Chance for a final walk so Skye could change clothes in the tent. He'd meant it when he'd said he'd go at her pace.

He bid goodnight to the guys and Kira and followed Chance into the tent. The soft glow from the lantern lit the small space. The dog circled his blanket twice, then settled down.

Skye lay on her left side, burrowed in the sleeping bag, her expression shy, watching him. He tugged off his T-shirt and set the ear plugs by his pillow. She lifted the bag for him to enter and gave him a glimpse of a pale blue tank top and matching sleep shorts.

He slid in, facing her, and his body responded to her heat and nearness. "Hi."

She placed her hand on his chest and his heartbeat sped up when she smiled and snuggled closer. "Feeling better?"

"You're here, so yeah." He traced his fingers along the curve of her hip and felt the lingering tension drain from his body.

Eyes on his mouth, Skye leaned in, lips parted. He met her halfway and with a teasing of his tongue and her nip on his lower lip, he lost himself in her taste. Nudging his knee between her legs, he fitted them as close as they could without him being inside her.

On a sigh, she lifted her head. "We should sleep. It's been a bit of a rough day for both of us."

He switched off the lantern, blanketing the tent in darkness, and slid his arm up her back. "I'm proud of how you handled the campfire."

"Having you with me helped." Skye shimmied until her head rested on his shoulder and she locked her right arm over his torso, keeping him close.

Holding her tight, he gave himself over to sleep.

He dreamed of the day Hunter had gotten shot. The explosions, the firefight, people yelling, Hunter bloodied and broken, and Damon saving their friend by becoming a human shield. But this time, Damon was mowed down too, and Aidan's limbs were frozen in place, held down by invisible weights, and he helplessly watched his friends die.

No!

A sharp bark startled him awake. He shot up to sitting. Heart pounding, he blinked down at Chance standing at his side, his large front paws pressing on Aidan's leg and Skye's stomach.

On a groan, she shifted the dog away and a second later, light flooded the space. She sat up him and laid her hand on his thigh. "Aidan, what's wrong?"

"Didn't mean to wake you. Sorry." He rubbed his hands over his face. Damn it, he hated when he had that dream again. *Hated* it.

She rubbed his back. "You're sweating and shaking. Bad dream? Want to talk about it?"

Chance whimpered, licking his hand then his face. He stroked the dog's fur while concentrating on breathing deeply. Somehow, Chance always knew to wake him from the nightmares. "It was the day Hunter was shot. Damon saved his life. But whenever I dream about it, I lose Hunter. And Damon. And I can't do a damn thing to save them."

"I'm sorry. That's awful." Supple arms came around him in a hug. "I dreamed about the fire for a long time. Sometimes, I still do."

Embarrassed, he reached for her hand. "From what you've seen so far on this trip, I'm a total head case."

Her fingers squeezed his fingers hard. "That's not

true. Things happened today and before today that showed we're both in need of some help, and lucky for us, we're able to help each other. I'm glad I can be here for you." She paused for a moment, eyes eloquent and earnest. "I care about you, Aidan. A lot."

The words dissolved his discomfort. He hadn't scared her away, not with any of it. How the hell did he get so lucky?

"Me too. In fact, I think I've fallen way past the caring stage." Needing her, he cupped the back of her neck and drew her toward him. The warm press of her lips and her soft sigh soothed him.

Chance pushed between them, knocking into their heads and licking them both.

Skye squeaked and leaned away, but her body shook with laughter. "Poor baby feels left out."

Aidan gave Chance a good rubbing and then tugged his dog toward the front of the tent and opened the flap. Hunter and Kira's tent was dark but light emitted from Damon's. He pointed in that direction. "Go to Damon."

The dog ran across the site and pawed at Damon's tent until the man let him inside. Damon gave Aidan a nod and then zipped his tent closed.

Aidan returned to his place beside Skye and gathered her close. "I wanted some privacy for this."

He grazed his lips along her jaw, then gathered her hair in his hands and lifted it off of her neck. He continued his journey along her neck and to the hollow at her throat and then lower.

"Aidan." She whispered his name on a sigh, and her hands grasped his shoulders.

He dragged his tongue across her skin, following the line of her tank top. When he reached the scarring on her chest, she stilled on an intake of breath. He lifted his head. "Is this okay?"

She gave him the sweetest smile. "I want you. I'm not going to pretend that I'm not nervous, but I want you anyway."

His heart did a funny little flip. She trusted him. Honored, determined to make her happy, he kissed her palm. "You're not the only one with nerves, baby. This is big. But it's going to be amazing."

Tapered fingers glided over his chest and then to his stomach and back again. "I love the way you feel."

Her hands on him were the best feeling ever. He had to return the pleasure. A moan escaped her lips when his hands journeyed up the sides of her body and around to cup her breasts. He slipped his hands under the fabric and continued the journey along soft, soft skin. Brushing his thumbs over her nipples made her sigh and press her hips into his body.

Skye reached for the hem of her shirt and with her gaze on his, slowly lifted the material and tugged it over her head and tossed it aside.

His breath backed up in his lungs. She was beautiful. He wanted to mark every inch of her body with his lips, to kiss every scar and worship every line and curve.

The scars covered most of her left torso and her arm. He traced the curve of her hip then higher once again to her breasts. Her breath caught again and she leaned into him, lips parted.

The kiss stole his strength. Skye was everything in that moment. He rolled her under him. Her hands drifted over his stomach and then lower, and Aidan's breath caught again when she grasped his cock in firm strokes. Desire fired through him at breakneck speed.

Her fingers tugged on his waistband. He eased his shorts over his hips and kicked them aside. Skye's hands found him again. He closed his eyes, and his head fell back. After imagining her touch for so long, feeling it along his bare skin was beyond amazing.

So amazing that losing control was in sight. Aidan pulled back and slid Skye's shorts and underwear down her legs, revealing the scars that covered her thighs. Laid out bare before him, she bit her lip and worry creased her features. If she thought he'd turn away, she was mistaken.

"Beautiful." Worshiping her with kisses and caresses, he glided over her calves, her thighs, and then worked his way to her center. Moving his weight to rest on one forearm, freed his other hand to slip into her folds. She was wet and ready and his finger slipped in easily.

She laid her hand on his arm. "More."

A second finger joined the first. Slow thrusts, as he kissed her, echoing the actions of his fingers with his tongue. Then he shifted away from her lips and kissed a path to her core. His fingers held her open as he teased her clit and then thrust his tongue into her heat. Skye gripped his hair and he felt her legs and hips shift in time with his movements. He wanted her so steeped in pleasure that fear and worry wouldn't have any room to bloom.

Her hands fisted tight in his hair, holding him close as her orgasm wracked her body. He kept going until he gave her a second one. Drenching Skye in pleasure quickly became his favorite thing.

Then he continued up her torso, covering her stomach and then her breasts with gentle sucks and teasing kisses.

"Every inch of you is beautiful. And if you doubt my words, you can't doubt this." He guided her hand to the heavy evidence of his arousal.

Soft hands wrapped around his cock. She worked his length, pushing him to the edge again. Her eyes locked with his and had a sheen of tears. "You really do want me."

"So much." He cupped her cheek and then lowered his head until their lips met.

Skye wound her arms around his shoulders and wrapped her legs around his waist. Holding her gaze, Aidan began to sink inside her perfect heat.

"Damn it. Condom." He raised his head and pulled back. His bag was within easy reach and he stretched over Skye to retrieve the packets he'd tucked into the side compartment on the chance they would find themselves in this very situation.

His hands shook as he rolled the condom into place. Skye stroked her fingers along his sides and then slid her arms around his torso and urged him down.

Aidan linked their hands together, and holding them by the pillow, he slowly pushed inside. Watching Skye's gaze darkened, he felt a deeper connection than he'd ever felt with anyone else.

Tight, wet heat gripped him. Fighting for control, he began to thrust.

He wouldn't last long this first time—she felt too good. She met his every movement, urging him for more. He increased the pace, spurred on by her pants and gasps. Sweat rolled off his skin, his heartbeat quickened, and a frenzied energy filled him.

When she clamped around him, his eyes rolled back. "Keep doing that, and I'm not going to last."

She did it again. "Can't help it. You feel so good inside me."

"Baby." Groaning the word, he shifted his position and angled in even deeper.

Her breath caught and her mouth opened and her fingers tightened on his shoulders. "Aidan."

Throbbing, he slipped his hand between them and worked her clit as he continued to thrust.

Electricity tingled at the base of his spine. He wasn't going to last. He moved faster and harder, until her pleasure crashed in a wave over them both and triggered his own release.

On a groan, he buried his face in her throat, breathing her in until his thundering heartbeat slowed. Skye's hands stroked over his slick back. He could fall asleep right there, just like that, but then he'd crush her. Bracing his weight on his arms, he pushed up and stared down at the face of the woman he loved. It was probably too soon to tell her how he felt.

She raised one hand to brush his hair off of his forehead. "Hi."

"Hi." He bent to kiss her. She had full hold on his heart, and he hoped she wouldn't want to let go.

CHAPTER TWELVE

Skye lay with her head on Aidan's shoulder. He stroked her back in long, lazy circles and she arched into his touch. "That feels good."

She didn't have to hide from him. Revealing herself had been one of the hardest things she'd ever done. But he'd made her feel beautiful, and for the first time, forget that she even had scars.

Loud barks broke the silence and didn't let up. Aidan shifted and urged her off his body. "Something's up. Chance never barks like that."

And then Damon's voice yelled, "Guys! Get up now. Fire!"

"Fire?" She sniffed the air. There was a hint of smoke.

He rattled their tent. "Move, now. It's big."

"Oh my God." Skye tugged on her tank top and shorts and shoved her feet into sneakers. Aidan finished dressing, and they ran outside.

Smoke sent a white veil through the air and flames coming from the cabin area sparked bright against the sky.

Her stomach dropped. Her arms and legs weakened and would not obey her brain's command to run.

"Called nine-one-one. We need to get these people out." Damon shined a flashlight toward the cabins. "Aidan, you're with me. The rest of you need to check tents and get people to the main road."

Fear more real than anything Skye had ever known made her blood run cold. She latched onto Aidan's arm. "You can't go into the fire. You could die."

He grabbed hold of her shoulders. "I know you're scared. I need you to be brave. I can't help people if I'm worried about you. I have to help check those cabins, baby, and you need to help check the tents. I'll meet you at the park sign."

She nodded. What else could she do? He pressed a hard and fast kiss to her lips and then ran off with Damon. She took a few running steps in his direction, but Kira thrust a flashlight in her hands. "Come on. We'll split the tents into three sections."

Skye licked parched lips. She had a job to do. Aidan would be fine… right? Most of the campers were already up and readying to run. The fire spread quickly, its crackling heat a steady reminder of how everything could change in an instant. Together with Kira and Hunter, she ran through the camp. Campers cleared free of their sites and ran toward the main road.

After all the tents were checked, Skye rushed to the

main road in search for Aidan. He wasn't at the park sign like he'd promised.

Kira and Hunter arrived. The rest of the fleeing campers staggered to a stop. After several moments, no one else arrived.

Still no sign of Damon or Aidan.

Flames blazed higher, catching some of the tree branches blowing in the wind.

If Aidan was trapped...

She tapped Kira's shoulder and yelled above the noise, "I'm going back. I have to find Aidan."

Not wasting time waiting for Kira or Hunter to respond, she ran in the direction of the flames. Ran toward the beast that had taken her down, and could have taken her life. It would not harm Aidan. She needed him.

She ran faster. Smoke burned her lungs. "Aidan!"

Twigs crunched under her feet. Sweat coated her body. "Aidan!"

Orange flames, angry and devouring, spread from one cabin to another. She dodged rocks and ran on. Her heart pounded, her muscles burned, and her lungs screamed.

The sound of a dog barking gave her direction. Chance had stayed with Aidan. She pivoted and ran through the trees toward the cabins on the far side by the lake. Hopefully, the path would stay clear.

Sirens wailed in the distance. That gave her some relief but not enough. Not until she saw Aidan.

"Aidan!"

She squinted in the darkness. Two figures moved toward her, led by a bounding dog wearing a flashlight. She shined her own light in their direction. When it hit Aidan's face, the adrenaline began leaving her system.

He and Damon carried a body between them. They reached her side in record time. She peered at the closed eyes. "Is he dead?"

"Passed out. Tons of liquor in his cabin." Damon grunted and shifted his hold. "We need to hurry."

The group moved fast through the camp, with Skye and Chance lighting the way.

When they broke through the trees, members of the fire department were on the scene, spraying water and battling the blaze. Two EMTs rushed to help Damon and Aidan with the unconscious man.

They reached the main road and Skye stumbled on shaky legs. Gratitude that she'd found Aidan alive and unhurt, dropped her to her knees.

As soon as Aidan was free, he spun and gathered her in his arms. "Are you okay?"

"I'm okay." She wrapped trembling arms around him. He held tight. "I want to go home."

"So do I." He cupped her face and raised her chin until she met his searching gaze. "I was so worried about you. What were you doing coming after us?"

She clung to his hard body, so relieved to have him close and whole. "You weren't at the sign. I was afraid something had happened, and I needed to find you, help you."

He bent and brushed her hair off her face. Emotions flickered in his dark eyes. "You ran into a fire for me."

"Well, not into flames. But I would have…" Realization of his words dawned. She'd faced her fear on pretty much the biggest scale possible. Her mouth dropped open, and she clutched his shirt. "Aidan."

"I'm so proud of you. You're stronger than you know, baby. And, that you'd do it for me…" He lowered his head, and she raised hers, straining for his kiss.

Her fear hadn't mattered when Aidan's fate had hung in the balance. She'd faced a fire for him and would have walked through one for him if necessary. And she'd do it again in a heartbeat.

Aidan kept his arm around Skye, and one hand wrapped tightly on Chance's leash. Firefighters finished battling the flames and police walked around taking witness statements. A news chopper flew overhead, its logo matching the news van and the microphone of the reporter who were on the scene.

When he and Damon were checking the cabins, all he could think about was Skye's experience, her emotions, and if anything was sending her back to a dark place. The fact that she'd faced her fear *for him* was more than he could fathom. Swamped in gratitude and love, he pressed a kiss to the top of her head.

One of the firefighters came up to them. "Thanks for

helping get people to safety. Homemade fireworks and drunken college kids are a dangerous combination."

Skye lifted her head. "Fireworks caused it? Not a campfire?"

"Stupid kids decided to add their leftover fireworks to their campfire. They just admitted it to the cops and to my fire chief. Thanks again to you and your friends for your help. The campsites have the all-clear now, so you can gather up your belongings." With a tip of his hat, he walked away.

"I can't believe it." Anger firing through his blood, Aidan turned to watch a few of the college kids head back to their cabins. Three of them had been taken away —two by the cops, and the one he and Damon had saved, via ambulance. But the rest walked, subdued, along the path leading to the campsites.

He'd taken one step forward when Damon and Hunter joined him, blocking the kids from his sight. Damon held up his hands in a *stop* gesture. "Don't go near them. Take a breath and relax."

"Relax? After what happened?"

"Yeah." Understanding in his gaze, Hunter patted Aidan's shoulder. "Because if you go over there, you'll likely end up spending the rest of the night in jail."

"Aidan?" Skye laced their fingers together and tugged on his hand. "Please. Come on, let's go pack."

He trooped back to the campsite with the others. Mood as dark as the night sky, he crawled inside the tent and over the sleeping bag. As he rolled the rumpled fabric, memories of his and Skye's time together cooled his anger. She'd really opened up to him—had trusted him with all of herself.

Skye crawled into the tent. A shy smile rose and she tucked her hair behind her ears. "Would you and Chance want to stay at my place tonight?"

He needed that. After the night they'd had, holding her would be the only way he'd sleep. From the earnestness in her expression, she needed him too. "I'm in. And I'm pretty sure we can talk Chance into it."

She laughed and kissed him, and they resumed packing up the tent and then helped the others break camp.

The reporter came over as they were loading up the cars. "One of the firefighters said you all helped get people to safety."

"My dog sensed it first, so he gets the credit." Aidan brushed off what they'd done. He wasn't a hero. He just wanted to go home.

"Has anyone ever brought fireworks here before?"

"Not in the four years we've been coming here. And I hope those kids learned their lesson. We're lucky the firefighters were able to contain the fire as fast as they were. This could have been a lot worse." They could have ended up in an inferno.

The reporter turned to Skye and his gaze tracked to her chest and arm, and the scars visible around her tank top and exposed by her tiny sleep shorts. She stiffened, her posture snapped straight, and she shifted away from his scrutiny.

Aidan moved fast, pulling her further into his

embrace. Twisting his body, he shielded her from view. He hadn't planned on talking about anything else with the reporter, but he needed the attention off of Skye. "You know, we came up here because I have PTSD and fireworks set it off. I thought this would be a safe place for me. You saw how many campers were here. People need to follow rules. I'm lucky I had my friends with me to pull me out of my episode, but not everyone is as lucky as I am."

"You're a veteran?"

He jabbed his thumb in Damon and Hunter's direction. "We three are. Maybe you could mention in your story that rules are in place for a reason. That's the important thing here."

Hunter gestured at the trees and brush around them. "It's also important not to set the forest on fire."

The reporter asked them a few more questions. Skye was quiet, but she leaned into Aidan and caressed his back. He appreciated the support, and memories of how she'd helped him earlier in the evening slipped into his mind. He was damn lucky to have her, too. He drew her closer.

Finally, the reported moved on to other campers.

Aidan spun in a slow circle, taking in the damage. Then he looked at the group. "I guess this place is out for next year."

He didn't want to chance another episode there, but more than that, he didn't want Skye to have bad memories about the fire.

Damon nodded, his features lined with grime, sweat, and determination. "Next year, we're finding an isolated cabin on private land."

Aidan cleared his throat and slung an arm around Skye's shoulders. Time to voice the idea that had been floating around in his brain. "Maybe I need to buy a place with plenty of acres around it."

"Vacation cabin? I'm in." Hunter grinned. "One big enough for all of us to be there together. We should have looked into that option years ago."

Kira nodded and slipped her hand in his grasp. "At least four bedrooms. And four bathrooms. Probably more. We can all go in on it."

Aidan rubbed Skye's back. She was too quiet. She was probably still thinking about the reporter and his blatant stare. "What about you? Think you'd like a private house with all of us?"

Her smile was hesitant, but there. "Um, sure."

She ducked away from him and pulled a sweater from her bag. After slipping it on, she tied another around her waist, hiding her thighs. Aidan wanted to throttle the reporter for making her feel bad.

During the rest of their clean-up, he tried to distract her and lighten the mood with question after question of what she'd like to see in the vacation home. The guys and Kira voiced their opinions, and Aidan had to laugh. Somehow, he didn't think a mountaintop beach resort existed. But they'd find something.

The camping trip had ended in disaster, but he had

his buddies, and he had Skye. And that was all that mattered. She was still subdued, but he hoped that returning home would help her relax. The only thing he wanted was to go to sleep holding her.

CHAPTER THIRTEEN

Skye woke early. Beside her, Aidan slept soundly. By the time they'd arrived at her house and gotten settled for the night, it had been after two in the morning. And she knew Aidan had lain awake for a long time, nearly as long as she had, while they'd held each other in the dark.

She rolled out from underneath his arm, climbed out of bed, and crept around Chance sleeping on the floor. Her brain needed coffee.

Making determined efforts to keep quiet in her own home was an odd experience. While her cup of full-strength coffee brewed, she pulled out the decaf pods she'd purchased for Aidan.

Cup in hand, she settled in her office and logged on to her computer to check for new emails from her clients. Two projects waited for her, but the deadlines were over a week away.

The sidebar of her news feed showed local stories

and events. Below the headline about Holiday's Fourth of July parade, another mentioned the fire at the campground. Skye clicked on the link. Hopefully, the cops and campground officials had found the rest of the kids who'd played a part in the fireworks.

The headline *Fireworks Cause Blaze* sat atop a picture of Damon, Aidan, Hunter, Kira, with Skye in the forefront. And at that angle—her left side—all the scars were visible. Front and center. For everyone to see.

Some of the comments mentioned her—the nameless woman with the scars. That was all she'd ever be.

Goosebumps dotted her skin. She glanced down, one regular forearm, and one covered in scars. Letting her guard down equaled exposure, which then resulted in pity or worse. She reached behind her for the long-sleeved, knee-length sweater hanging from the back of her chair and tugged it on, covering all of the scars. But she still felt naked, violated, and ashamed.

The article called Aidan a hero. Of course, he was a hero. They mentioned his military service and his PTSD, and his request that people follow rules.

Aidan was a hero, and she was a coward.

She'd never be comfortable enough around strangers. Hell, it had taken her forever to warm up to Kira and the guys. And even now, she still had bad days. And with Aidan too, there were still moments of worry. Small moments, but still there.

She'd never be able to conquer her fears.

Never be good enough for Aidan.

Too weak. Too messed up. Too much an emotional wreck.

He'd grow tired of constantly reassuring her. He'd eventually move on to someone less high-maintenance.

He needed someone whole, someone strong, someone who wouldn't let him down.

And that someone wasn't her.

Footsteps padded through the hall, along with Chance's nails clicking on the wood floor. Aidan's voice floated from the kitchen, followed by the sound of the back door opening. She stood at the window and watched Chance race around the yard. Saying goodbye to Aidan also meant saying goodbye to Chance. How hard it would be to lose them both. Not to mention Kira. She couldn't expect Aidan's close friend to remain friends with her. It looked like once again, she'd be all alone. She didn't want to be that closed off woman anymore. But it was for the best. Aidan deserved to have someone who could be normal in public and not-so-public situations.

Aidan came through the doorway, coffee cup in hand, hair mussed and wearing a sleepy smile. "Hey. Thanks for getting the decaf."

Her heart broke.

She set her coffee on her desk and tugged her sleeves over her hands. "We need to talk."

His smile disappeared. "What's wrong?"

"I can't... I..." She wrapped her arms around her middle. "I'm sorry, Aidan. I can't do this anymore."

"What do you mean, you can't do this?"

"This. Us. It's… not working out."

"The hell it isn't." His coffee cup hit the desk with a thud, and he towered over her. "What happened between last night and this morning to change your mind?"

She glanced at her computer, and he followed her gaze right to her picture on the screen. His features softened, and his hands cupped her shoulders. "Baby, I'm sorry."

She stepped back until he lowered his arms. "No. I am. This photo. Me. It brings everything to the surface. I can't be what you need. I'll never be normal."

He raked his hands through his hair. "We're both scarred. Maybe mine are on the inside, but they're still there. The difference is, even knowing that I'll never be back to the way I once was, I'm not too scared to live again. I don't want you to be too scared either."

"You need someone whole."

"I need you."

"This was a mistake. You'll grow to hate me."

"I love you. And I think you love me too." The stubborn glint in his eyes dared her to deny it.

Her heart stuttered its beat.

He loved her?

He wouldn't say it if he didn't mean it. Aidan didn't lie.

Happiness wove through her heartache like ribbons of warmth. She couldn't deny her feelings or ignore her fears. Letting go hurt so badly. "I do love you, and that's why I want what's best for you."

"You're what's best for me. You know what I see

when I look at you? A warrior. A strong woman who carved out a whole new life for herself."

"I ran away from home. That makes me a coward."

"But you ran here. And we found each other. What you've been doing with me is brave. Letting me see you, letting me touch you, letting me in."

Fear rose as a lump in her throat. "I'm not naive enough to believe you won't get tired of telling me the scars don't matter."

He clasped her hand and gently pulled her toward the door. "Then it's time you believed it."

"Where are we going?"

"Upstairs." Holding her hand, he brought her into the spare bedroom where they'd dropped off their bags the night before and stopped in front of the full-length mirror resting against the wall.

Skye shook her head as an inkling of what he intended to do dawned. "Aidan…"

"See? Beautiful." He stood beside her, stroking her shoulders. "You have to believe it. I want you to say it."

For long minutes, she stood there, gazing at her reflection, unable to speak.

"Look at your eyes, your hair, your face. See how strong your arms and legs are, how sexy your body is with those killer curves. But besides that, you're kind, warm, big-hearted, funny, and very sweet. You're stunning, beautiful, inside and out and everything I've always wanted."

His words touched something deep in her soul. Tears ran down her cheeks. She sank to the floor. Sobs wracked her body even as strong arms wrapped her in an embrace. She couldn't stop the flow. All of the hopes and fears and self-loathing and pain poured out in every breath and every tear.

Aidan held her through it all.

Finally spent, she pressed her cheek against his chest. Her throat was raw and her head was pounding. So many times, she'd examined her scars with a mixture of loathing that they existed, and gratitude that they weren't as deep or widespread as they could have been. But she'd never looked at them and found them beautiful.

Aidan had.

Screwing up her courage, she raised her gaze to the mirror, and slipped off her sweater. And looked. Really looked.

Jagged bumps and discoloration covered areas when smooth, tan skin had once been. No, she didn't look like her old self, but they showed that she'd been through fire, and more important, that she'd survived. Maybe she'd survived so that she'd meet Aidan and be able to help him. Fate worked in funny ways.

"See? Beautiful." He curled around her in solid, steady support. "You have to believe it. I want you to say it."

She studied the combination of smooth and scarred skin. The road to recovery had been a painful, slow process. Physically, mentally, and emotionally. "I'm beautiful."

"Again."

Trying to see herself through his eye, the words became easier to say. "I'm beautiful."

He cupped her chin and raised it until he pierced her with his sincere gaze. "I don't want someone else. I want you. I don't care if I have to tell you a hundred times a day that you're beautiful. I'll never get tired of it, or you."

She reached for hope and strength and found both when she clasped his hands. "You said you need me. I need you too. We've been taking care of each other."

"That's what people in love do." His tone was mild, but his eyes were intense, dark, and full of urgency.

In them, and viewing her reflection there, she had her answer. "I love you, Aidan."

His eyes closed for a moment. When he opened them, they had a wet sheen. "I love you, Skye. The road might not be easy, but we can handle anything together. Stay with me?"

"I promise." She leaned back to accept his kiss. The words were easy when her heart did the talking.

EPILOGUE

Aidan sat in his home office, staring at the diamond ring in his hand. Having Skye with him through the entire summer had been amazing, and she'd all but moved in with him. As much as he enjoyed their almost living together, he needed a more permanent arrangement.

He'd had the ring for a few days. With every moment that passed, the urge to propose grew stronger. But Skye deserved the most perfect proposal he could give, and for all of his brainstorming, he hadn't come up with "perfect" yet.

"Ready to go?" Her voice sounded behind him.

The ring box tumbled from his lap to the floor. He closed the ring in his fist and kicked the box under his desk, and then turned his head toward her. "Sure. I'll be right down."

Rather than leaving, she came further into the room. She'd wound her hair into a messy bun that showcased her long neck. "What were you doing?"

His thoughts spun. The perfect proposal wasn't her catching him unaware and redhanded. He bolted to his feet and shoved the ring into his pocket of his swim trunks. Smiling at her, he hoped he didn't look guilty. "Uh… Just working on a proposal. For work. It can wait. Let's get to the party."

The Labor Day pool party at Damon and Kira's parents' house was an annual tradition. This year would be the first he was bringing a date. Skye wore a white cover-up that concealed her skin from neck to knee. He wasn't sure what she wore underneath. She'd been noncommittal about it for weeks. Would she be comfortable enough to try a bathing suit or would she wear the cover up the whole time? He didn't care if she wore twelve layers or if she wore two. As long as he had her, he'd take her any way at all.

Chance's barking from the kitchen drew Skye's attention. She slipped her arm through Aidan's and led him toward the door. "I feel bad about leaving him here. We'll have to take him to the park tomorrow to make up for it."

"Right." Sweat trickled down his neck and his heartbeat pounded in fast beats. If she brushed against his thigh, she'd possibly feel the ring.

Chance continued to bark. The dog stood by the window, attention focused on a squirrel.

"Hey boy," Aidan called, clapping his hands. "Want a treat?"

The dog's ears pricked at the word and he trotted over to greet them. Aidan grabbed a treat from the cabinet, knelt and held it out. It was gone in seconds. While he gave the dog a good belly rub, he wracked his brain for some excuse to return to his office. But Skye had seen that his computer was off, and they'd turned the lights off as they'd exited the room. And his wallet, phone, and keys were by the front door.

Skye rubbed Chance's head and smiled at Aidan. "You ready to go?"

He cast a glance around the room and an idea sparked. "Did you pack extra sunscreen?"

"Yep. All set."

His hopes for sneaking back to the office while she grabbed the sunscreen from the upstairs closet plummeted. Hiding the ring in his bedroom wasn't an option, not when she shared drawer space. And wandering through the spare bedroom while she waited downstairs wouldn't work either, not with the way the floorboards squeaked.

His phone pinged with a text. One hand over his pocket, he rose and headed for his phone.

Damon: Where are you guys? You're never late. Everything okay?

He glanced at the clock and did a double take. He'd spent more time mulling over the proposal than he'd thought.

Skye walked toward him, slipping her purse strap over her shoulder. "Kira texted me before I came into your office. She was wondering where we were. I guess we're the last people to arrive. I hadn't realized I'd taken so long getting ready."

She brushed a hand along the seam of her cover up. Her fingers trembled the barest bit.

Concern rushing in, Aidan caught her hand in his. "You okay? If you want to skip the party, we can."

"No. I want to go." Uncertainty clouded her gaze but her voice was strong. She nodded, to emphasize her words, or maybe in an attempt to convince herself, or him.

He tightened his grasp. "If that changes at any time, just let me know, and we'll go."

They'd hit some hiccups in their months together, but they'd weathered those spots with honesty and communication. He could trust her to let him know when she was uncomfortable, and she could trust him to tell her when he was stressed, and they could do so knowing that the other person always had their back.

She nodded again and smiled. "I love you."

"I love you too." He bent and kissed her. Warm lips met his, and the subtle scent of cocoa butter from Skye's sunscreen filled his senses.

Holding his hand, she drew him toward the door. "Let's go."

With the dog settled and watching them, and Skye ready and smiling, he couldn't stall in the house a moment longer. Pocketing his wallet and phone, he followed, and then pulled the door shut behind them. Maybe he could give Damon or Hunter the ring at the party, and they could hold it at one of their homes for safe keeping until his plans were set.

During the drive, they heard one of the two radio

commercials Skye had voiced for the toy company. The days she'd come to the office with him had filled him with extra energy. He was so proud of her and her work.

She grinned. "Hey, it's me."

As her voice flowed out of the car speakers, and she smiled happily beside him, love welled so strong in his soul. He didn't want to wait another minute to propose.

After they parked in the driveway of the Kallis home, he laid his hand on Skye's thigh. "Ready?"

"I am." Her fingers traced a pattern on the back of his hand. "Thank you for always making sure I'm okay."

"I always will."

The front door opened and Kira came out, smiling and waving as she walked toward them. Skye gave his hand a squeeze and then unbuckled her seatbelt and grabbed her purse. She had her door open and was outside and greeting Kira before he had a chance to say anything further.

"Aidan, you can go right around to the backyard." Kira pointed toward the side of the house, where music and laughter echoed. "I need Skye to help me with something really quick."

Skye kissed him. "I'll meet you in the yard."

After one more kiss, he followed the path into the decorated yard and spied Hunter and Damon by the side of the pool. He threaded his way through the crowd to join his friends. There were plenty of umbrellas for Skye to sit under. The engagement ring nearly burning a hole through the material, he rested his hand over the pocket of his swim trunks. No way would he be able to think about anything else until he asked her.

Damon glanced over his shoulder, toward the house. "Where's Skye?"

"With Kira. She'll be out in a minute."

Hunter regarded him over the top of his sunglasses. "You seem restless. Things good?"

"Sure." He felt for the ring again and tried some deep breathing.

Damon's brows narrowed. "They're obviously not good. What's wrong?"

Aidan shoved his hand through his hair and fought the urge to pace. "I'm proposing to her."

"That's awesome. She's good for you. You're good for her. Do it." He grinned and slapped Aidan on the back. Then his gaze dropped to Aidan's hand secure over the pocket. "Wait—do you mean right now?"

"I was looking at the ring when she walked into my office, and I had to stuff it into my pocket so she wouldn't see. I wanted to plan the perfect moment. I only intend to do this one time, so I want to get it right, but I don't think I can wait another second to ask."

"You love her, so no matter how it goes down, it'll be great, okay? So don't worry." Hunter patted his back and then raised his beer in a toast. "Oh hey, here she comes."

Aidan turned, heart in his throat. Skye walked through the yard. She paused under one of the umbrellas and waved to him.

His heart smiled. And his nerves faded away. He

faintly felt pats on the back from his friends once more. Then he walked toward her, amazed again that he'd found her and beyond grateful that she loved him too.

She pulled at the drawstring tie around her waist and then pushed the wrap off her shoulders. It fell to the ground in a puddle of white.

She wore a bikini.

Bright red.

Hugging her curves.

Among a sea of fifty party-goers.

His mouth dried. His heart pounded. His body hardened. With quickening steps, he dodged people until he stood in front of her. Her gaze was latched onto his, but she seemed confident and calm.

Cheeks pink, she bit her lip for a moment before her mouth curved into a smile. "What do you think?"

He had to touch her. Had to hold on to the best thing that ever happened to him. Hands unsteady, he cupped her shoulders. "I think you're amazing. And beautiful. And brave."

"You helped me feel that way. Thank you."

"I'd do anything for you. You mean everything to me. I love you."

She slid her hands up his chest and linked them around his neck. "Me too. More than words can say."

He couldn't have asked for a more perfect moment. Heart pounding, he withdrew the ring and the backed up a step. His heart leaped when her gaze dropped to his hand. "I want you, always. Will you marry me?"

Her eyes widened, and her gaze darted from his eyes

to the ring and back again. She threw her arms around him in a tight hug. "Yes."

The fierce emotion in her voice echoed the emotions swirling inside of him.

He pulled back enough to slip the ring on her finger. It sparkled in the sunlight, mirroring the way she lit up his life. "I'm so glad I found you."

Skye cupped his neck and urged his head down to meet hers. "Me too. And I'm never letting go."

A grin spread across his face. He'd have her with him for always.

As their lips touched, a sense of peace, of happiness, of completion, filled him.

With Skye, he'd found everything he needed.

Thank you so much for reading *More Than Words*! If you liked it, please leave a review. Reviews help other readers find my books.

Don't miss the other stories in the Holiday Hearts series:

Kiss Me Again

Kira Kallis is newly thirty, tired of being single, and wants to find someone special in time for Valentine's Day. After spending years focusing on her career, she has a great job, and supportive family and friends, but life as the perpetual third wheel is lonely. Creating an online dating profile was the easy part. Navigating the lines between truth and illusion in her "matches" is a lot harder.

Hunter York has been friends with Kira for years. From morning runs to chats over coffee at the office, he loves the time they spend together. But it can't go further than that. She's his best friend's sister, his co-worker, and off-limits for too many reasons. When he learns that she's using a dating site, he insists on checking into her matches who draw too many questions and yield not nearly enough answers. Overprotective or not, he cares too much to risk anything happening to her.

The more time they spend together, the harder it is to deny their connection and chemistry. Kira begins to wonder if the perfect match could have been by her side all along, and Hunter struggles with what could happen if he discards all the reasons he's wrong for her. But taking that step means going beyond paper hearts and chocolate-flavored kisses. It could mean risking a friendship they've both grown to depend on.

All I Want

Damon Kallis is always in control, whether in his VP position for his family's toy company, captaining his men's rec league hockey team, or taking care of his friends. There isn't any room for romance in his well-ordered life. He made that mistake once, and it nearly cost him everything. Work, family, and friends are all he needs.

All Emily Lombardi needs is a job. After her ex poisoned her reputation as a reporter, no TV station is willing to give her a chance. When the job as Damon's executive assistant opens up, she's in the right place at the right time. Landing the position is simple compared to dealing with Damon -- the stubborn man won't let her in.

Working in close quarters leads to accidental touches, lingering glances, and simmering passion. Soon, they can't deny their attraction.

With the holiday season under way, Damon's ice starts to thaw, and Emily sees someone caring and real, someone she could count on. But their past experiences are hard to forget, and when their new-found love is tested, only a Christmas miracle can give them a happily-ever-after.

Marry Me

Join Kira and Hunter from Kiss Me Again, Aidan and Skye from More Than Words, and Emily and Damon from All I Want as they say their I do's.

. . .

Kira and Hunter have been planning their wedding for months. When their venue goes up in smoke two months before their big day, they are left scrambling to find a new location.

Engaged for four months, Skye and Aidan have held off on making wedding plans. Aidan fears that Skye is getting cold feet, but Skye's reluctance stems from her mother's overbearing behavior. Still, she can't put off the wedding forever. She just wants a way to celebrate without the focus being so much on herself.

And newly-engaged Damon can't wait to marry Emily, but her family is insisting on a wedding venue that's booked solid for the next three years. He's not happy about waiting but doesn't see a way around it. Emily longs for something more unique and personal but is afraid to hurt the family by breaking with tradition.

When Emily recommends her favorite vacation spot as a substitute venue for Kira and Hunter, moving the wedding from Holiday, NY to Virginia Beach, VA, Damon sees an opportunity to solve all three couples' problems—a triple wedding.

But a March nor'easter bearing down on the East Coast the weekend of their wedding spells disaster for the couples. And that's only the beginning.

Find all the books in the series:

https://www.susanscottshelley.com/holidayhearts

ABOUT THE AUTHOR

USA TODAY bestselling author Susan Scott Shelley writes romance with heat and heart that celebrates love without limits. She enjoys watching hockey, training for her next run, reading romance novels, and binging episodes of her favorite British TV shows. Susan lives in Philadelphia with her husband and also works as a professional voice over artist. A city girl who likes being out in nature as often as possible, she has yet to meet a plant she hasn't wanted to take home and she really wants a pet crow.

Vist her at https://susanscottshelley.com

ALSO BY SUSAN SCOTT SHELLEY

Philadelphia Power series

Against the Rush, Over the Top, Behind the Mask, From the First, Powered by Love (series collection)

Love & Rugby series

Spiral, Spark, Smolder, Shine, Surprise, Swoon,

Love & Rugby vol.1, Love & Rugby, vol.2, Love & Rugby, the complete collection

Love & Rugby: Season of Love series

Savor, Seduce, Stay,

Love & Rugby: Season of Love, the complete collection

Pride of the Bedlam series

Skating On Chance, Holding On Tight, Scoring Slater, Playing with Pride (series collection)

Buffalo Bedlam Series

Making His Move, Fighting For More, Taking His Shot, Playing to Win (series collection)

Game of Love series

Rekindled, Captivated, Enamored, Game of Love (series box set)

Holiday Hearts series

Kiss Me Again, More Than Words, All I Want, Marry Me, Holiday Hearts (series box set)

Rocked by Love series

Love Notes, Love Song

The Philadelphia Frenzy series

Mad Scramble, Hometown Hero, Team Spirit

Bliss Bakery series

Sugar Crush, Heart of the Batter

The Falling series

Falling Faster

Other Novellas

Simmering Ice, Flirting on Ice, Iced (series box set) Tackled by the Girl Next Door

Sign up for Susan's reader newsletter, and never miss a new release:

https://www.susanscottshelley.com/newsletter

www.ingramcontent.com/pod-product-compliance
Lightning Source LLC
Chambersburg PA
CBHW071347170626
46811CB00003B/1016